ROGUE CODE

ALSO BY MARK RUSSINOVICH

Zero Day

Trojan Horse

ROGUE CODE

Mark Russinovich

THOMAS DUNNE BOOKS
ST. MARTIN'S PRESS ✹ NEW YORK

THOMAS DUNNE BOOKS.
An imprint of St. Martin's Press.

ROGUE CODE. Copyright © 2014 by Mark Russinovich. Foreword copyright © 2014 by Haim Bodek. All rights reserved. Printed in the United States of America. For information, address St. Martin's Press, 175 Fifth Avenue, New York, N.Y. 10010.

www.thomasdunnebooks.com
www.stmartins.com

Library of Congress Cataloging-in-Publication Data

Russinovich, Mark E.
    Rogue code : a Jeff Aiken novel / Mark Russinovich. — First edition.
        pages ; cm
    ISBN 978-1-250-03537-0 (hardcover)
    ISBN 978-1-250-03538-7 (e-book)
  1. Cyberterrorism—Fiction.   2. Suspense fiction.   I. Title.
    PS3618.U7688R64 2014
    813'.6—dc23

                            2014008414

St. Martin's Press books may be purchased for educational, business, or promotional use. For information on bulk purchases, please contact Macmillan Corporate and Premium Sales Department at 1-800-221-7945, extension 5442, or write specialmarkets@macmillan.com.

First Edition: May 2014

10 9 8 7 6 5 4 3 2 1

ACKNOWLEDGMENTS

This book was made better by the discussions and invaluable feedback I received from readers of early drafts. I'd like to thank John Walton, David Cross, Chris Jackson, John Lambert, Scott Field, and Matt Thomlinson, colleagues of mine at Microsoft, who shared their real-world experience fighting cybercrime and improving cybersecurity in their detailed and thoughtful reviews and discussions. Thanks also to Jeff Prosise and Ron Watkins, friends of mine outside of Microsoft, who gave me their perspectives as fans of the techno-thriller genre.

Haim Bodek deserves a special thanks for the information he shared with me, initially and unknowingly via his Web site, book, and participation in documentaries on HFT that I researched, and then later after I contacted him, in our long conversations over Skype and in the comments he gave me on book drafts. I'm grateful for his foreword, which sets the tone perfectly for the book. His position as an industry insider and pioneer of market microstructures makes his warning that HFT poses risks to our economy when looked at as not just low-latency algorithmic trading that can spiral out of control in algo-vs-algo trading, but as including the secretive-order types that give insiders unfair advantages, something that we should all heed.

I also want to thank my agent, David Fugate of Launch Books, for his staunch support of the Jeff Aiken books series, and also for helping me secure the sale of its movie option. Peter Joseph, my editor at St. Martin's Press, did a fantastic job of guiding the book through to publication, even somehow compressing rigid publishing schedules to hit target dates when my day job got in the way and slowed my delivery. Thanks to Melanie Fried and to the editorial production staff at St. Martin's Press for their painstaking passes over multiple drafts of the manuscript, somehow finding typos and grammar mistakes in passages that I read dozens of times.

Finally, I want to again thank the real-life Daryl, my wife, for indulging me in my many hobbies, of which novelist is just one. Her patience and support for my crazy schedule and her smiling face, which greets me when I get home from work or finish a multi-hour writing session, provides the emotional foundation for my creative endeavors.

FOREWORD

When I first read *Rogue Code*, I thought, "Here is a thriller that is really tuned into the dangerous potential of electronic trading." Mark Russinovich paints a picture of what most would consider the nightmare scenario of what could go terribly wrong in the U.S. stock market. It is a dystopian view of where electronic capitalism might lead us.

And yet, *Rogue Code* shows us a Wall Street which is all too familiar—think it a synthesis of age-old business practices that thrive on exploiting the grey areas of financial regulation *and* modern electronic trading systems whose *opacity* is the only thing keeping computerized criminals at bay. The end result is a fictional portrayal of a global-market system that is hauntingly familiar in both its vulnerability and its propensity for financial crisis.

Mark is impressive, detail-oriented, hands-on. He aims to introduce you to the technical mechanisms, hacks, and exploits that are longstanding practices in the field of cybersecurity that he rightfully associates with critical vulnerabilities in our national market system. More importantly, Mark has tied together two disciplines that must cross-pollinate: cybersecurity and computerized trading. After you have read *Rogue Code*, you will believe these two fields are on a collision course.

Still, I confess that as I read *Rogue Code* I couldn't help but smirk inappropriately at times. *If he only knew*, I thought. As the financial crisis proves, often Wall Street itself can be its biggest threat.

Rogue Code is a work of fiction. The bad guys don't run multibillion-dollar hedge funds that have institutionalized illegal insider trading into a business model. They don't run massive Ponzi schemes affiliated with unusually successful trading companies. They don't publicly brag about their multi-year zero-loss trading days fueled by "secret sauce" that only recently has caught the attention of regulators.

In my experience, the current threat to Wall Street isn't going to come from abroad . . . it has already firmly embedded itself into the fabric of our marketplace.

We don't need foreign agents to compromise our markets. We are quite adept at causing the flash crash and more than *twenty-five thousand* "mini flash crashes" all by ourselves.

We don't need a foreign agent to rig an exchange to provide a benefit to an affiliated trader—we are quite adept at creating conflicts of interest, self-regulation of for-profit entities, and regulatory loopholes that naturally evolve into collusive arrangements.

We don't need super-hackers planted where they can exploit the order matching code for their own benefit, as the most lucrative career path for a developer is to cycle from exchange to trading company, back to the exchange space, and then onward to the most elite trading firm having attained the "goods."

And I should know. Over a decade ago, I was awarded my first major promotion at a major investment bank for exploiting a back door in a European electronic exchange to get prices faster. Back then, we discovered holes. At some point, the game changed, and the industry started creating holes.

The search for what we in the industry call an "edge" led exchanges to manufacture artificial advantages in order to satisfy their most-favored clients. What else differentiates an exchange, when the primary service that traders want is to extract a profit in what nearly always is a zero-sum game for short-term traders? The money has to come from somewhere, doesn't it?

And so many years later, I decided to blow the whistle on high-frequency trading to regulators, citing numerous undocumented features designed by exchanges to accommodate high-frequency trading strategies at the expense of the public customer. It was the road not traveled for one of my background.

Mark is an outsider to high-frequency trading, but that is what makes his contribution all the more sobering. What if Wall Street lost its stranglehold on a system where complexity and volatility equate to trading edge? What if outsiders indeed targeted the very systems which regulators readily admit they cannot monitor or control in any meaningful manner?

And that is probably the most terrifying conclusion one can draw from

Rogue Code. Wall Street, having grown so accustomed to exploiting and circumventing its own system, is dramatically unprepared for real enemies, those who have no stake in the bedrock of our capitalist system.

—HAIM BODEK
MANAGING PRINCIPAL
DECIMUS CAPITAL MARKETS, LLC

MEMORANDUM

DATE: October 13

FROM: Walter D. Winterhalter
Inspector General
Office of the Inspector General
U.S. Securities and Exchange Commission

TO: Eleanor Kaschnitz
National Security Advisor

RE: Concern

I wish to personally express my deepest concern about the possible intentional or inadvertent disclosure of the actual events that occurred last month, regarding the New York Stock Exchange Euronext. The potential for incalculable harm to our financial institutions and the world financial system is extreme. While speculation is rampant in the media, both traditional and electronic, the diverse nature of the speculation tends to cancel out fears, though the attention has had a dampening effect on the trading public. Only the passage of time will inform as to what extent. For now, I must urge in the strongest possible terms that no official account of events be made public and that every step possible be taken to prevent a credible source from leaking what we know and are learning.

I cannot emphasize this more forcefully.

cc: POTUS

DAY ONE
MONDAY, SEPTEMBER 10

NYSE EURONEXT SECURITY REACHES NEW LEVEL

By Arnie Willoughby
September 10

Bill Stenton, director of NYSE IT Trading Platform Security, has confirmed a roll-out of new security measures designed to make trades within the Exchange the most secure transactions in the world. In public comments Saturday, Stenton said, "There are two realities in security trades in the 21st century. The first is they must take place with great rapidity, as this is a digital world and traders will settle for nothing less. The second is that trades must occur within a system that is completely secure. We believe the NYSE Euronext system provides both of these [requirements]."

He went on to describe in general terms the scale of the measures now routine within the trading platform's software. Special software continuously seeks out anomalies as well as attempts at penetration. "The software is continuously updated to keep it current and to provide the best trading platform possible. To assure its near seamless operation, we are constantly searching for what we call hiccups in the system. These [hiccups] appear most often when we are merging new subsystems with existing ones."

Regarding attempts at penetration, Stenton admitted that the problem is ongoing. "We have the most sophisticated security system in the world. I cannot recall a single instance in which anyone penetrated our first wall, let alone the subsequent security measures. You can trade with absolute confidence."

Asked about the recent appearance of a common malware bot on one of its Web servers, Stenton dismissed the incident as insignificant. "The security of the system was never in doubt." Despite Stenton's assurances, knowledgeable sources expressed reservations. "The presence of a bot on a public site of this significance should be a wake-up call, but I fear it is not," said one informed source who asked to remain anonymous.

Henry Stolther, a frequent NYSE critic and publisher of the *Stolther Report,* responded to Stenton's comments, focusing on the speed of trades within the system. "The NYSE has moved too rapidly into accelerated trading," he said. "The Exchange is competing in a highly competitive industry and wants to make its system as user-friendly as possible. As a consequence, certain abuses now possible with current computing power have gone largely unregulated."

Asked if he was referring to high-frequency traders, Stolther said, "Absolutely."

READ MORE: STOCK EXCHANGE, NYSE, TRADING PLATFORM, SECURITY

US Computer News, Inc.

1

WATERFALL GLEN FOREST PRESERVE
DARIEN, ILLINOIS
8:13 A.M.

Vincenzia Piscopia, known as Vince to his American colleagues, sat on the cool gray boulder, feeling more than a little strange. He'd never done this before and was now having second thoughts. He glanced about the small clearing. He was alone. Maybe I should just go back home, he thought, pretend this never happened.

Vince was thirty-four years old and had spent his entire life in the digital age. Though he hiked as often as possible, he was a trifle overweight and soft. Computers and the Internet had always formed an integral part of his life. He even made his comfortable living as an IT operations manager for the New York Stock Exchange, working out of the Chicago IT office. Originally from Milan, Italy, where he'd been employed by Siemens, he found he enjoyed America more than he'd expected. His only real complaint was of his own doing—he just didn't get out very often.

Vince had always been a nerd, and social media formed the greatest part of what passed for his social life. He tweeted, maintained two blogs—one on life in Chicago for an Italian expat, the other about computer security, a particular obsession of his—and he'd been one of the first 100,000 to have a Facebook account. He'd seen the value of Toptical from the beginning and had opened his account almost from the day the company launched. Between his iPad, iPhone, and home computer, it seemed to him that when he wasn't sleeping or working, he was social networking.

Even on his long solitary hikes, he brought along his iPhone and had a connection nearly everywhere. He wasn't alone in that regard. Just the week before, he'd hiked some six miles on this very trail, found a lovely spot to take a meal, and while sitting there had checked for messages. Just then, he'd heard a chirp. Not twenty feet away, he spotted a woman of middle years answering her cell phone. He'd just shook his head at the incongruity of it all—then texted a few replies of his own.

But today was different. Vince was here to meet someone. It was all very twenty-first century, he'd told a colleague at work. And while for others this sort of thing happened from time to time, for Vince it was a first. As a result, he found himself fretting about his appearance. He'd been honest with the photographs he posted on Facebook, and Sheila had assured him that she was as well.

He wasn't concerned, though he knew that Facebook friends were often disingenuous in that regard. He'd know soon enough if Sheila was the stunner her photos showed, or a fake. If the latter, they'd hike a bit, and then, once he returned to his apartment he'd unfriend her. That would be that.

And he'd never do this again.

It was a bit cool for September, but Vince liked the typically brisk Illinois autumn. He found it invigorating and at moments like this, on a remote trail far from the popular routes, he could imagine himself back home. He was getting cold and zipped his Windbreaker up higher. From nearby came the gentle murmur of a stream.

It was Sheila who'd suggested they meet on a Monday when there'd be few hikers and that they take this moderate hike in the DuPage County forest preserve. He'd been pleased that it was one she knew about, since it was already his favorite. The nine-mile trail snaked around the Argonne National Laboratory, the loop passing through rolling woodlands and savannas, the contrasting scenery adding to the charm. Though all but within the Chicago suburbs, the preserve had a very rural feel.

The main trail was layered with crushed gravel, and it crested a few difficult hills. There were usually hikers such as himself, joggers, and those training for marathons. The only negative was that horses were permitted on the wide pathway, and they brought with them their unique problems; which was why Vince preferred the smaller side trails where the horses didn't go.

He heard movement and turned with anticipation. But instead of Sheila, there was a man, another hiker. Vince smiled and nodded a distant greeting. The man nodded back and continued toward him.

Their exchanges had started just the week before. Sheila was the friend of a friend on Facebook. She lived in Chicago and also worked in IT. A few messages established how much they had in common, so they'd switched to e-mail. Sheila had spent a summer in Europe after university, backpacking locally in some of the same places Vince knew. She took her work in software security seriously, and from the first complimented his blog. She'd never been married and had no children. In fact, she'd never even lived with a man, she told him. Like Vince, she worked long hours, and at twenty-nine had decided it was time to get out more.

The other hiker stopped where the trail widened. He was tall, physically fit, with fair hair. He placed his foot on one of the smaller boulders and slowly retied his shoelace. When finished, he lifted the other foot and repeated the process.

Vince thought about the man's presence for a moment, wondering if it was good or bad. Sheila had suggested this quiet location off the main trail for their first meeting, hinting for the first time at the possibility of romance by mentioning how she often came here alone, wishing someone special were with her.

He chuckled at his thoughts getting ahead of reality. He was about to see a woman he'd first met on Facebook, that's all. The other hiker meant nothing. You don't have a private romantic rendezvous on a public hiking trail, he told himself.

Vince scanned back along the trail and saw no one new. He frowned, pulled out his iPhone, and checked for messages. Nothing.

He glanced up. The hiker was finished. He smiled as he approached the Italian, looking as if he were about to say something. That's when Vince spotted the heavy branch held loosely in his hand.

"Have you seen this?" the hiker asked just as he reached Vince.

Vince looked up into the man's face, then quickly at the upraised branch and only in that final second of his life did he realize what the branch meant.

2

In the dimly lit room, the frosty glow of flat-screen monitors bathed their faces in a silver light. One of the men licked his lips in anticipation. The other stared keenly at his screen as his fingers raced across the keyboard.

They'd been at this for three intense weeks. Neither had said as much to the other, but both believed that today they'd succeed in penetrating the New York Stock Exchange trading system—at last. First they'd speculated over whether it was even possible. For the last few days, they'd been certain it was.

Once they infiltrated the system, they'd be free to do anything they desired. They'd be able to change whatever they wanted at will, free to bring trading to a halt, free to let it run amok, free to alter billions of dollars in transactions—free to loot any account, anywhere, with impunity and in secret.

Theirs would be digital financial power of nearly unimaginable dimensions. And their electronic trail would be hidden within tens of millions of lines of code and terabytes of monitoring and audit logs.

For all the time they'd worked on this assault, it was not so long as each of them had spent in previous similar operations. Though access and speed were vital components of the Exchange, so too was security. It was essential that its digital walls be perceived as impenetrable, and so the Exchange presented itself to the trading public as a model of security. It could afford the best and brightest and claimed to employ only the most up-to-date and finest security technology.

Which, of course, was nonsense. The so-called walls resembled those of a fortress castle of the Middle Ages, designed and constructed to withstand any siege. Until the invention of the cannon, such fortresses had rarely succumbed to so direct an attack. Instead, when they fell, it was most often because of a vulnerability to an assault team, often no more than two or three men, who found their way beneath, over, or around the outer wall, then through the subsequent protective labyrinth until they'd identified a weak point and exploited it. With that access, they'd leverage the security open and admit the besieging army.

So it was for them as well—except that they were both the assault team and besieging army folded into one.

For these last weeks, the two had probed, managing to approach the core of the NYSE Euronext network from every angle their skill and knowledge allowed. When their efforts had proved a dead end, they retreated and tried again.

But the time had not been wasted, for they'd established which servers they could reasonably expect to compromise. They then spent hours scouring internal Web sites and file servers, scanning documents, spreadsheets, and group user directories. Using bits of information—some from a file here, others from a report posted on a team collaboration site there—they'd determined who in the company had access to these same servers, how they accessed them, and what systems they used.

The work had been tedious, but they were well suited to it, and the time passed quickly. And despite all the setbacks, days of them at a stretch, there'd been steady progress. A fragmented view of the internal organization of the Exchange and its IT infrastructure emerged, like a jigsaw puzzle only partially complete. Systematically they gathered, analyzed, and cataloged every piece of information and document they encountered, as they couldn't know what detail might prove helpful to them in time.

Once they'd mapped promising paths through the system to their goal, they attempted to inject themselves into points on those paths. In that, they'd had help. Vulnerabilities in software the Exchange used were publicly reported, so instead of crafting a hole on their own, they explored to discover a zero day opening or if the Exchange had failed to patch any bugs. They'd found no zero day opportunities but did find vulnerabilities in at least one application used internally by the Exchange. Their continued efforts led them to code written by FirstReact, a cybersecurity research company that discovered and reported bugs to the Exchange for a substantial fee.

Even then, their attempt at penetration failed with the first three servers they'd targeted. But they persisted and at last hit upon what they'd sought, what they'd been certain would exist if only they persevered. One of those well-educated, highly paid, bright minds on the NYSE Euronext IT team had yet to seal a vulnerability. That was all they'd needed to ooze through the inner workings of the Exchange's network, and from there it hadn't taken long to locate a path to the doorway of the trading engine systems. Today, as anticipated, they'd managed to plant their code on that doorway known as a jump server.

Neither had said a word when they realized what they'd done. It was in many ways a sublime moment, best savored privately. After a short pause, one of them began to determine the extent of their penetration, as there was much yet to be done, more barriers to surmount, a complex of security measures to bypass. It would all be demanding, but they had the lever bar in place. When they pressed, it would create a yawning hole they'd exploit relentlessly. Finally, with a sigh of satisfaction, one of the men pushed himself back in his chair and said, "We've got them."

"That was too easy," the other answered, reaching for a fresh Red Bull.

"You know, we shouldn't be able to do this."

"That's their problem." He leaned forward. "We still have a long way to go yet."

Their next step was to establish access known only to them, a simple means to gain entry even after the portal they'd just opened was closed. Known as a backdoor, it would allow them ready access up to the jump server. After the backdoor was installed, they spent several hours setting up a command and control system for their personal use. It would be the external platform from which they could conduct their operations.

In the past, attackers had been compelled to compromise legitimate servers or establish business accounts with hosting companies that rented out servers. Both options were problematic because traffic to outside servers could be suspicious and because renting a server usually required a legitimate credit card. Now, with the advent of public cloud computing, they could instantly establish a trial account using nothing more than a burner cell phone number and set up a free command and control server anonymously.

Next, the pair planted within the system their own carefully crafted code, software that would allow them to remotely send program commands. Those commands, taken as genuine by the system, would enable them to do anything—absolutely anything—once they had full access.

"So," the taller one said to the other, "just how rich do you want to be?"

3

I'm going to see Ryan now!" Connor Stern all but shouted at the shocked woman as he barged by her desk, storming up to the closed door of his broker's office and pushing it open.

Ryan Kramer looked up, startled. "Connor, I'm—"

Stern slammed the door shut behind him. "You know why I'm here! Don't pretend you don't!" He raised his fist above his head. In it he clutched several sheets of paper.

"Connor, sit down. There's no need for a scene. I can explain it all."

"That's what you said over the phone. Well, that isn't going to work! I'm entitled to answers. More importantly, I'm entitled to my money and I don't intend to leave without it!"

The telephone rang. Kramer hesitated a moment, then picked it up, gesturing at the chair in front of his desk. Stern appeared to compose himself before taking the seat, and he leaned forward in agitation.

"No," Kramer said. "Just bring us some water." He replaced the telephone, then sat back in his chair. "That was Vivian. You scared the hell out of her. She's afraid to come into the office." He looked at the man evenly. "Connor, you need to get control of yourself or I'm going to have to call security."

"Security? I was with your dad for eight years and never had a complaint. When you took over he asked me to stay on, so I did out of respect for him. When my wife and I came to you thirteen years ago and told you our retirement plans, you wrote up this very impressive proposal, with an investment arc that got us where we needed to be. Well, I'm sixty-eight years old now. I had a mild heart attack last month. It's time to cash out while I still can. We talked about this last week when I gave you the sell order. You of all people know how tough it's been since the crash, that I've had to work three years longer than I wanted. I should be on the beach in Florida right now, planning my next fishing trip."

Just then, there was a light rap at the door. Kramer's secretary entered, glancing nervously at Stern. She carried two glasses of water, which she set on coasters on the desk before quietly retreating. Stern licked his lips, then reached forward to take a glass. He was a big man, perhaps thirty pounds overweight, with thinning gray hair and a ruddy complexion. He took a sip, then a long drink before placing his glass back on its coaster.

"You know it's been hard for me," he continued. "I've run up over a million dollars in debt to keep the company going. I laid off everybody I could. I've got a daughter who won't talk to me, because I had to let her husband go, and he can't find work. I've even had to use my own assets as collateral. I'm upside down in a house I owned free and clear eight years ago. I've worked seven days a week to dig myself out of this hole I'm in, one I never caused." He looked at Kramer, no longer visibly angry.

"We talked, Ryan," he continued. "We talked a long time before I decided to pull the plug. I needed two million. According to the workup you did, we were supposed to have more than five by now. Okay, I understand that you can't guarantee a rate of return, that you don't control the stock market. I get that. Nothing's certain in this world. We were way down, but when we crawled back up to two million, the missus and I talked. Sell now and we still had some time to retire before old age did us in. I could pay off the debt, give Uncle Sam what I had to give, and we'd have half a million left. That's not much, not nearly enough for the life we wanted, but it would do. With that money we can buy a cheap condo near Miami, draw on the rest when we had to, living mostly off Social Security. That was the plan. Not much, but we could live with it. Ryan, I told you all this." Stern raised his fist. "Then you send me this!"

Kramer spread his hands before him defensively. In a measured voice he said, "I didn't do this to you, Connor."

"You told me two million! That's what we were going to get when you executed the order. That's what you promised!"

"I make it a practice never to promise, Connor. I gave you the prices of the stock in your 401(k) and told you the figure if we executed the order at those prices."

"That's right! And I said do it! It wasn't easy settling for so little. Every dollar over a million four was money in our pocket, money to retire on."

"I understand." Kramer glanced at his wristwatch.

"Do you? I don't think you do. You sit in this fancy downtown office, punching numbers, running spreadsheets, taking your cut. A business your father gave you. You never worked a day in your life to build it up! Tell me, Ryan. You're not making any less now than if I'd got the full two million, are you?"

"I . . . I'm getting less. I'd much rather see you get the figure we talked about."

"'Figure we talked about'? What's that? It was two million dollars! Not some figure. It's my life here. My life!"

"Connor, I executed the order," Kramer said testily. "I sent you the statement."

"One million five hundred twenty thousand. That's what I've got here." Connor shook the papers in his fist. "That leaves just over a hundred thousand after I pay my debts. Then there's your fee, odds and ends. I ran the numbers, Ryan. Fifty-two thousand dollars. That's it. No half million. What the hell happened?"

"The sells were supposed to go at specific price points, but the record shows they were executed later than that and at a much lower price. This happens from time to time," Kramer added archly. "The stock market is volatile. It's in the paperwork we gave you. It's just the way the stock market works."

"I'll bet the big boys never have it happen to them. No, they get theirs. My order was at the back of the line and got the scraps. You promised me!"

"I never promise."

"You know what fifty K means to me? Nothing! Absolutely nothing! Maybe we can buy some crummy one-bedroom condo with it. Then we get to scrape by on Social Security, eating dog meat. Medicare's not free, you know. I've still got to pay, and pay through the nose."

"You can always file for relief."

"You mean bankruptcy? You're a moron, that's what you are. I wish I'd seen it sooner. If I file for bankruptcy, I'll be tied up in court for two years at least. Two more years of snow and ice. I don't even know if I'll be alive in two years! And the lawyers will take every penny I've got." Stern slumped back in his seat. "It wasn't supposed to be like this. It wasn't."

Kramer stared at his watch pointedly.

"Hell," Stern said in sudden surrender. "Why am I all worked up? With my ticker in the shape it's in, I haven't got much time anyway."

4

Jeff Aiken's shoes slapped the track as he picked up his pace for the final mile. It was good to be running again, good to breathe fresher air, good to be away from the busy Manhattan streets, even if only within the illusion of Central Park.

He followed the old Bridle Path of the Lower Loop because he enjoyed its beauty and because his feet and knees liked the forgiving dirt. He ran steadily, passing a few slower runners, yielding to others. Though hugging the reservoir, from time to time he caught a striking view of the park.

He closed his mind to all thought, focused on his body, the rhythm of the run, the sensations of pain and pleasure that coursed through him. Seeing the end within sight, he kicked into his final sprint, his side aching and his lungs a bit ragged from his recent inactivity. He pressed himself hard.

More than ten years before, Jeff lost his fiancée at the World Trade Center. Working then for the CIA, he and his team had uncovered clear indicators of the pending 9/11 disaster. But when he met with his superior, he was unable to persuade him or anyone else to act. He even failed to save Cindy's life, though he'd known she'd be in Manhattan on the probable day of the attack.

They'd spoken just moments before her death.

The experience was devastating. Afterwards he'd left the CIA to start his own cybersecurity company as he struggled to deal with the tragedy.

Jeff was born the youngest of two sons. When he was six years old, his parents and brother were killed in a two-car accident. He'd been with his grandparents at the time and remained with them thereafter. They were loving surrogate parents. Jeff's elderly grandfather died when he was a sophomore in high school, and his grandmother passed when he was in college. Until Cindy came along, he'd remained largely a loner.

He'd gone on to obtain his doctorate and then taught at Carnegie Mellon before joining the Cyber Security Division of the CIA's Information Operations Center. Though he spent most of his time before a computer, he'd played rugby at the University of Michigan and worked to stay fit.

When he'd next been in Manhattan, he went to Ground Zero at the start of the new construction, drawn there by deep emotional currents. But seeing the gaping hole, the busy construction, had offered nothing except painful recollections. Over the long decade following her death, his memories had slowly dimmed, though there were moments when some reminder would bring back the sharp pain of loss.

Now his work had drawn him to Manhattan once again.

He'd loved Cindy deeply and was sure he'd never experience such a relationship again. But later, during the frantic chase to stop a planned al-Qaeda cyberattack on the West, he formed an unexpected bond with Daryl Haugen. He'd known her as a colleague for several years, and both of them were surprised by this development, as neither had been looking for a companion.

He and Daryl had entered into a passionate affair that blossomed into what each believed was a lasting relationship. She'd left the United States Computer Energy Readiness Team, known as US-CERT, where she'd headed a team and served as assistant executive director of the Computer Infrastructure Security Unit at the Department of Homeland Security, or CISU/DHS, before joining him. He'd formally organized his cybersecurity company, calling it Red Zoya, the name coming from the zero day applications used in the al-Qaeda attack. They'd set up their lives and business in a Georgetown town house.

Following the climactic events in Turkey the following year, Daryl was briefly hospitalized. It had seemed to him then that the chronic separations that previously marred their life together had come to an end. During the time of their recovery from their injuries and wounds, Jeff came to believe that a full and lasting love had blossomed within both of them. Working together, they were a unique and highly regarded team. It seemed to him an ideal life, joined as lovers and professionals.

But they were each often consumed by their work. One or both of them was frequently absent on assignment, and even when they were together at the town house, they were heavily involved with the business. Daryl had assured Jeff that she would make their relationship a greater priority, and for a few short golden days it seemed she would. But their intended month-long vacation in Italy after her release from the hospital in Turkey was cut short within a week when an old colleague had called Daryl, desperate for her help. Unable to do the job on the road, she flew back to the States and that had been that.

Afterwards, nothing changed. They rarely saw each other, and when they were together it was as if they weren't. Jeff raised the subject of their relationship again and Daryl reassured him—again—but finally he decided they had no future, not like this. His had been a rational decision, though not an easy one. Continuing as they were wasn't healthy for either of them. He'd seen other working couples go on as they were for years, never remaining connected at the most important level, interacting with each other superficially, as colleagues at work, their sex life little different from a coupling with a stranger. They both deserved better.

This wasn't what he wanted. He'd hoped that presenting her with what was in effect an ultimatum would jar Daryl into reality, cause her to carefully examine her priorities. But when he finally managed to get her attention and a bit of her time, the conversation had not gone well. Initially, Daryl had given another assurance, and then, realizing how serious he was, she turned angry. Finally, when the inevitability of his position became obvious, she became stoic.

Jeff was disappointed and unhappy that she'd chosen to disconnect rather than put their relationship first. It seemed to him that Daryl thought the relationship was going okay and had been offended that Jeff would accuse her of not being committed. From his perspective, she should have been able to see what was taking place. It could not have been more obvious to him. He was deeply frustrated that he couldn't get her to acknowledge it. All he really wanted was for her to understand that she needed to make a decision, needed to make the right decision for them. But that wasn't how she'd taken it.

In the end, before he felt they'd really discussed things, she abruptly moved out while he was on assignment, taking her possessions. She'd given him the benefit of the doubt with those acquisitions that could reasonably be considered jointly theirs, her fairness just one of the many things about her he loved. Her move was impulsive, he thought, something else about her he loved, though not when he was on this end of her actions.

The tragedy, if that wasn't too strong a word for it, was that it had been obvious to Jeff that she cared about him as much as he still cared for her, but regardless, their life choices drove them relentlessly apart. And though it was his hope they'd remain friends, he couldn't see them ever getting together again as a couple. Someone would come along in either of their lives, and in time the other would receive a wedding invitation. He'd seen it with former couples he knew and now accepted that fate as his own. In seeming confirmation, Jeff and Daryl had not talked in the year since the breakup.

Ironically, Jeff's reaction to that life change had been to throw himself into work with even greater zeal. During those hours he wasn't working or asleep, he was most often at the gym. He'd taken up tae kwon do, finding he enjoyed the physical contact and flexibility it gave him. One of the unintended consequences of Daryl's departure was that he was in the best shape of his life.

But despite the efforts of attractive women to start something new with him, Jeff had so far declined. He simply couldn't take that next step. He'd given it considerable thought but didn't understand why he was stuck. He found himself wondering about Daryl. Was she dating? Living with someone already? He didn't know and felt he shouldn't try to find out.

5

Daryl Haugen stared at her computer screen. She heard the clang of the cable car on California Street and looked out her bay window. The route was a block over, but she never grew weary of the sound. It was like a siren call.

Fog blanketed her street. She peered into it for a moment, trying to make out the row of apartments across the street, taken once again with how thick the stuff could become in so short a time. Moisture collected on the outside of her window, forming heavy tear-shaped drops that began to creep downward as she watched.

In her first months in the city, she'd found herself often taking the cable car for no reason other than the experience. Though the line was popular with tourists, she soon learned that half the riders were locals. She got to know them by sight, though no one much talked to each other—except the tourists. They just never seemed to shut up.

She'd not changed everything about how she lived. She still carried pepper spray, and three mornings a week, she found time to continue personal workouts with an emphasis on defense training. It didn't matter where you lived, you still had to be responsible for yourself.

She turned back to her screen. She'd brought work home as usual. This was a contract job for a Midwest insurance company. She was designing an update to its cybersecurity systems that would include antivirus, host-intrusion detection, network monitoring, anomaly alerts, and operational lockdown. She had employed some of the new techniques she learned in her time with Jeff. In fact, she often realized, her time with Red Zoya had been helpful, which was only one more reason for her anger at the change imposed on her.

She'd been on this project for some weeks and expected to be at it another two months. She'd just returned from an on-site week at the corporate headquarters, where she worked closely with the company's IT and cybersecurity teams, designing the architecture for the solutions she'd devised. It was best to keep things as similar in design and appearance as the system the company was now using. That consistency was often the most difficult part of a project like this. While on-site, she'd assisted the IT squads in picking vendors for the new cyberproducts her revised system required. As she neared completion, she'd perform the final, and key, function of guiding the new system's deployment and making it operational. She wasn't exactly saving the world, but the work was challenging and occasionally satisfying.

Daryl had been required to deal with the usual problems she encountered as an attractive single woman in her field. Software engineers were typically men, and their female counterparts often tended toward the plain. Daryl was an exception and had come to view her looks as an inconvenience. Her mother was a beauty as well, and they'd talked about the challenge more than once over the years.

Slender and just over average height, with a fair complexion and blond shoulder-length hair, Daryl stood out. She was a natural athlete and skied at every opportunity. Encouraged by attentive parents, she'd early discovered a natural affinity for language, and by the time Daryl was a teenager, she spoke Spanish, Portuguese, and Italian fluently. Her parents were convinced she'd become a linguist, but Daryl also enjoyed mathematics and computers.

She'd been admitted to MIT at seventeen, then completed her Ph.D. at Stanford while living at home. With a world of career choices before her Daryl had given serious thought to what she should do. She'd briefly considered applying to the FBI as the idea of chasing bad guys held a strong appeal, but instead she'd gone to work for the National Security Agency, which had a greater use for her particular skills. The NSA intercepted communication of all types in order to develop intelligence information. To accomplish all that, they relied extensively on computers. Her background, including her command of languages, made her a natural. After several years she moved to the Department of Homeland Security (DHS), where she could be more proactive developing and coordinating defenses for the country's rapidly expanding cyber-infrastructure.

Daryl checked the time on her screen. She'd have to stop soon. She'd agreed to meet someone for coffee. God, she hated these meet-ups friends were constantly arranging for her. During the first months after moving to San Francisco, she'd refused them all, then reluctantly acquiesced. Yet still she wasn't ready. No, she'd come to realize that the last thing she wanted right now was a man in her life. She was still trying to get over the last one.

That's what comes from thinking it was true love, she'd told her mother one day. She'd thought just being herself and living the life she wanted would have been enough for Jeff. He'd certainly seemed to say that to her. They got along well; the sex was wonderful. Later she'd decided that compatibility had blinded her to specific realities. Core issues existed in every relationship, and in ignoring them, she'd also disregarded the most basic rules.

As far as she was concerned, Jeff could go to hell. He might be handsome, charming on occasion, faithful—which was a rare enough quality in any man these days—a hard worker, but in the end, she'd found him cold-blooded. That was the hardest part for her, the way he'd thought it all through without a word of warning to her and then just sat her down one Sunday night when she'd been exhausted from three grueling weeks in Vancouver. It was clear that they weren't going anywhere, he'd said in that steady voice of his, that continuing as they were wasn't good for either of them. It was time to recognize the reality of the situation.

Then he said he hoped they'd stay friends.

That had almost been too much. But she held back her anger, told him that if that was what he wanted, it was just fine with her. She had other options. He was leaving the next day to work in Dallas, and in anger, she told him she'd be gone when he came back.

They'd spent that night in separate bedrooms, and tired as she was, she found it difficult to sleep. Finally, well after midnight, she drifted off into a fitful slumber. She'd found it hard to discriminate between her restless dreams and those long moments when she drifted, not awake but not asleep either. Once it seemed to her that a form had stood in her doorway—Jeff, she thought. He'd said nothing, stood there unmoving, a comforting presence; then she drifted off. When she next came out of sleep, he was gone, and when she awoke in the morning, she found he'd quietly left on his trip without another word.

She'd called Clive Lifton that same day. He was a longtime friend to both of them as well as a colleague. Though it had just fifty employees, his San Francisco company, CyberSys, Inc., was highly regarded in cybersecurity, providing both training and consulting. Clive was a diffident man of middle years, a bit scholarly in his manner. He also was the creator and perennial sponsor of CyberCon, a modestly sized but popular event for those specializing in cybersecurity. Clive ran the conference as an indirect way to advertise his company and its services to the security community.

Both Jeff and Daryl frequently traded information with him concerning attack techniques as well as swapped cyber community gossip. He'd tried to hire them more than once. Now she called to take him up on his standing offer. San Francisco was just about far enough away from Washington, D.C., as she could get, and Daryl thought the profound change in culture would do her good.

To her surprise, Clive tried to talk her out of making the move. "You and Jeff are special," he said. "Don't do anything you'll regret. You aren't going to do any better, Daryl, neither of you is. Stay put, give this some time, rethink your priorities. Work is always there, but what you two have, at least from my perspective, is wonderful and worth a bit of sacrifice."

But his recommendation had been shared to no avail. She'd told Clive this was Jeff's decision and that he was talking to the wrong person. Finally, they agreed to terms and Clive had offered to help find her an apartment. Daryl carefully packed her few things, surprised she'd accumulated so little during her time in Georgetown, and then driven cross-country in three exhausting days, her anger toward Jeff hardening with each passing mile.

What most pissed her off, what really made her mad, was how much she still cared about him.

Clive was true to his word and located two apartments for her, either of which would have been just fine. She'd taken this second-floor one on Pine Street in Lower Pacific Heights because of its 1913 architecture and lovely bay window. On clear days, light bathed her small living room, turning it aglow. She'd placed her workstation there, and when she worked at home, she let the sun wash over her as she listened to the clanging of the cable car bell and the moan of the foghorn in the bay.

That was one of the many things she had to adjust to, the way one part of San Francisco could be holiday sunny, while another was shrouded in gray fog. When she went for her frequent walks, she always took a light jacket with her since she managed to pass through at least three microclimates every few minutes. She loved it.

The offices for CyberSys, Inc., were located in a remodeled Victorian home off Sutter Street, between Nob Hill and Chinatown. A brass plaque beside the entrance placed there by a local historical society authenticated that the address had once served as a brothel. Its various rooms were divided into no more than three cubicles each. Still, spending time there was like working in her aunt's turn-of-the-century house. The hardwood floors glistened and the woodwork never failed to catch her eye. She loved the high ceilings, and Clive, she learned for the first time, was something of a horticulturist. At least he filled the place with plants and managed to keep them thriving when he wasn't staring at a computer screen.

The city itself was different from Georgetown, with its own history and culture, and that, along with the new working environment, had been just what Daryl needed. She was already acquainted with two of the employees and soon found that she knew several others by sight. Clive ran a pleasant operation free of drama and even managed to have a fair share of extroverts among his employees. They had all taken an immediate liking to Daryl and were the ones now setting her up for romance.

She supposed she could bring those efforts to an end if she really wanted to, but some part of her thought that meeting new men was the way to drive Jeff from her memory. Not that there'd been so many. She put in long hours and traveled at least once a month. It was the nature of the work. She'd asked Clive to keep her on the coast and in the West, and he agreed without comment. Distance was another key, she'd told her mother, who she came to realize disapproved of her breakup as well.

Daryl checked the clock again and reluctantly closed her laptop. She sighed. Maybe tonight over coffee, she'd stop wishing the man across the table were Jeff.

DAY TWO
TUESDAY, SEPTEMBER 11

NYSE SUPER HUBS CRITICIZED

Critics Allege Secret System Vulnerable to Attack

By Dietrich Helm
September 11

On the anniversary of the 9/11 attack on the World Trade Center, a new report from think tank Bearing Institute warns that our financial system is more vulnerable to terrorism than ever. The NYSE is building super trading hubs around the world through which an ever-increasing percentage of all worldwide securities trading will pass. The computer engines within the hubs are the most powerful ever conceived, and they are all vulnerable to terrorist attack, the report claims.

The report argues that a well-placed bomb could bring any of those hubs, the precise location of which NYSE keeps secret, down with disastrous results to the world financial system and that backup systems aren't sufficiently powerful to carry trading load and that many transactions would be lost if the primary systems were disabled. If a timed simultaneous attack brought down more than one hub at the same moment, the damage to global finance would be catastrophic. The NYSE, critics charge, has needlessly exposed itself in pursuit of profits.

Manning Benting, former SEC director, argues that the NYSE has no choice but to construct super hubs. Computers and the connecting infrastructure have made it easier to create any number of international trading exchanges. All those new markets are in direct competition with the traditional exchanges. One response to competitive trading markets is systematic consolidation. Another is to build the super hubs. "The Exchange really has no choice if they plan to remain the major world player," Benting said in response to the Bearing Institute report. "If they don't do it, someone else will."

It is projected that the bulk of those secret super hubs will be operational within five years. They are designed to be indispensable to any significant trade, anywhere in the world. Even if a trade were to take place outside the NYSE system, some of its elements must pass through one or more of the Exchange's super hubs, incurring access fees as they do so. NYSE is a concentration of potential financial influence never previously known.

The problem Benting points out is that by consolidating the flow of data through a handful of key physical locations, the NYSE exposes itself to physical attack. Such an attack could come from a warring nation or from terrorist organizations. "We must keep in mind that the attacks on 9/11 were directed at the World Trade Center in New York City," Benting said. "The financial underpinnings of the Western economy remain a prime target for them [al-Qaeda]."

The irony is that the Internet was created by the United States Department of Defense to have maximum redundancy in the event of nuclear attack. The network is based on spreading the flow of data to as many different routes as possible. If any portion is taken offline, the others will take over.

The NYSE is taking the exact opposite approach.

"They are doing this for economic reasons," accused one critic, "not to safeguard the world financial system. We trust them with our assets when by their actions they demonstrate they are undeserving of that trust."

TAGS: MANNING BENTING, BEARING INSTITUTE, NYSE EURONEXT, SUPER HUBS

Cyber Security News

6

COPACABANA BEACH
RIO DE JANEIRO
12:41 P.M.

Victorio Manuel da Silva-Bandeira—or Victor Bandeira, as he more commonly called himself—took in the sweep of the azure South Atlantic through his Chopard sunglasses and estimated he'd take another hour in the sun and sand.

It was a warm spring day in Rio, the temperature approaching eighty, with a light wind off the water. The sky and sea were so closely matched in color as to blend into one. The majestic Sugarloaf Mountain commanded the landward view.

Bandeira sat in a low white lounge chair protected by an expansive umbrella. Beside him on the sand were a rumpled beach towel and a small table for drinks and food. Bandeira sighed contentedly as he set an empty beer bottle down. It had been too long since he last did this. As a boy, and later as a teenager, he'd spent every day he could on the beach. What had happened?

Life, he thought, life is what happened.

Spread across the fine sand was the usual crowd for this time of year: couples, pairs of friends, residents of the hotel, and the occasional family. Around the point was Ipanema beach. There the beach was carefully, though informally, sectioned off—couples here, teenagers there, families in this place, sports enthusiasts playing on their stretch, the entirety of the famous expanse demarcated for organized use.

Copacabana was different, had always been different. Extending along its stretch across the street were the resort hotels, the beach before them designated as exclusive territory by modest flags. No intruders, no roaming packs of disruptive youths, no vendors in irritating numbers. Each area was meticulously maintained and carefully serviced by attentive hotel staff.

The only exception to the rules of beach occupancy was made for lovely young women, who were always welcome. This was, after all, Brazil. From his chair, Bandeira tipped his head to more carefully examine the two women lying on oversized beach towels not that far away. He'd wondered about them at first, but when his bodyguard, Paulinho, standing between Bandeira and the roadway, shook his head lightly he decided they were exactly what they appeared to be—very attractive women taking in the sun. It was the national pastime of Brazil, for rich and poor alike, especially in Rio.

Beyond them, Sonia, Bandeira's current mistress, rose from the water and stood there a moment, moving her long blond hair onto her back, then met his gaze with her bright dark eyes. Of primarily German stock, Sonia was Brazilian about the eyes and in the languid manner of her every motion.

Bandeira's yacht, the *Esmeralda*, was in dry dock. Otherwise, they'd have spent the day aboard her, but this beach was very nice indeed. Bandeira made a mental note to visit it more often. He turned to summon a waiter for another beer. As he did so, he caught a glimpse of the Copacabana Palace Hotel, the oldest premier resort in South America. Built in 1923 when the tunnel through the mountains from central Rio opened up Copacabana beach and what became the South Zone of the city, the structure, with its distinctive art deco design, was now a national landmark. Almost anybody who was anyone had spent time here: the rich, the famous, royalty, movie stars, millionaires, billionaires, and the grifters they drew. The hotel had been remodeled and extended but remained from the beach as unchanged as the day it went into operation.

Unlike in modern hotels, you actually felt as if you were living in luxury when staying at the Palace. The only irritation from Bandeira's perspective was that thus far, his attempt to acquire a penthouse on the top floor with a view of the beach and sea had been rebuffed. Well, he thought, if money doesn't talk, there are other ways.

Sonia had come over to stand beside him, her firm legs dominating his view, droplets of water sparkling on her lightly tanned skin, pretending to shiver as she toweled herself dry, making a *brrr* sound with her lips. Then she smiled—always an invitation there—before lying back on the beach towel, squirming this way and that, her breasts commanding his attention as she made herself comfortable. "The water is very refreshing," she said. "You should go in." As she slipped on her sunglasses, her pretty face assumed the aspect of an innocent child.

"Soon." It was pleasant here with the sun and warm sand. The water would be cold.

The waiter arrived with his Bohemia beer and glass balanced atop a small silver serving tray and held it down for Bandeira, then vanished when the beer alone was removed, taking the empty bottle with him. Bandeira took a pull, instinctively glancing down at his stomach and wondering where they had gone—his youth and fitness. He'd been a slender young man, one who always took his vitality and vigor for granted. Over the years, with greater personal and financial success, he'd slowly filled out, first into a man of stature, now into one of advancing years with too much fat.

Despite the excess weight he was a handsome man, just above average height for his generation, a bit darker in complexion than the upper class of Brazil, with gleaming teeth behind fleshy lips. He wore his lustrous, mostly black hair combed straight back. Occasionally when he smiled, there was just a touch of cruelty about his mouth, the hint of something more sinister than his usual pleasant demeanor suggested.

Bandeira had no illusions about Sonia. At fifty-one years of age, he knew his appeal lay with his bank account. He'd seen more than one man in his place make a fool of himself over a woman like her—a girl, really. He wasn't about to play that game—or be played.

Still, her affection seemed genuine enough, and with the exception of telling him that her ambition was to become Miss Brazil, she'd never asked him for a thing, absolutely nothing. Of course, they'd been involved only a few weeks. That self-suffiency could change.

Sonia came from a good family, one of the oldest if no longer the richest in the country. She knew other wealthy men. In fact, her father would have been very happy if she'd shown an interest in nearly any of the rich men with whom he worked. It was still traditional and common in Brazil for the young daughters of the wealthy to marry men who were contemporaries of their fathers. Such arrangements were mutually profitable to everyone concerned. Through such a marriage her father, Carlos Lopes de Almeida, long president of the Banco do Novo Brasil, would unite his family with another powerful and affluent family. The patriarchs would share the same grandchildren, who would in time inherit. His daughter would be assured of a life that continued in the style in which she'd been raised. All would remain as it was.

Bandeira wondered what Lopes de Almeida would think if he knew about the two of them. He smiled at the thought. He wondered even more just how much of Sonia's interest in him was a youthful act of rebellion against her father and his traditional ways; certainly more than a small measure. Not that it mattered. He gazed at her and speculated what she'd think and do if she knew his real history, where he'd come from.

"What are you smiling at?" she asked.

He hadn't realized she was looking at him. "Nothing."

"Mmmm. I'll bet it was something."

I'll tell her, Bandeira decided. I'll tell her the whole story and just watch. That, he thought, easing back in his chair, will be something. Better yet, he reconsidered, I'll show her.

7

As Jeff Aiken and Frank worked in their assigned office on Wall Street that morning, Jeff reflected on how this assignment had come about. He was contacted two months earlier by the director of Trading Platforms IT Security for the New York Stock Exchange and had negotiated the terms of the project as well as the start date. The two had never met, but as was often the case, Jeff's reputation preceded him, and his name came up by word of mouth. A common bot had been discovered on one of the Exchange's Web servers, and security had no idea how it got there. The breach should have been impossible.

The director was Bill Stenton, a handsome African American man whom Jeff estimated to be in his early forties. Before meeting, Jeff had done his usual background research and learned that Stenton had been with the Exchange just three years, having come from the IT department of Wells Fargo. Though Stenton was reportedly competent, some of the feedback Jeff got characterized the director as high-strung and even difficult at times.

Jeff couldn't help noticing that though trading platform security was a major component in maintaining the integrity of the world's most important financial trading institution, there were three layers of bureaucracy between Stenton and the CEO. That was just one of several indicators to Jeff that the Exchange, despite all its computer and software dependency, didn't give its core system's security the attention it required.

When they met, Stenton told Jeff that his IT team was of the opinion that the trading platform had not been targeted specifically by the malware bot, but rather the NYSE site had been accessed by an automated scan searching for a vulnerability. Finding one, it had infected the system. The bot didn't appear to have impacted any customers or disrupted operations, but there was concern because it had managed to get past the security team's defenses, and it had been on the server for at least three days before IT stumbled across it while performing routine software upgrades on the system. If something as straightforward as a bot could make it into NYSE's computers, then certainly malware far more dangerous could break through as well.

"We regularly run internal red team versus blue team exercises, but I'm concerned that we're overlooking obvious weaknesses," Stenton said evenly. "What we want is an external penetration test, the very best and most sophisticated you can manage. Our suspicion is that one of our own employees inadvertently opened the door for this bot. Pull no punches. I want you to be sneaky as hell. Learn our exposure and tell us where it is so it can be fixed. Our own people won't even know what you're up to. It is absolutely essential that the integrity of our trading software not be subject to question. The stability of world financial markets depends on it."

"Pentests" were the cybersecurity equivalent of military war games, designed to evaluate the security of a computer system by simulating a malicious attack from outsiders as well as insiders. Once the pentest was completed, its results were presented to the system operator. The report included an assessment of the system's security and vulnerability along with specific recommendations to counter them.

The pentest itself involved an analysis for gaps that were usually a consequence of inadequate system configuration, hardware or software flaws, or other operational process weaknesses or lax security countermeasures. Those conducting a pentest approached the computer system as a potential attacker might and sought to aggressively exploit any security holes they discovered. Those chinks in the armor could include misconfigured and unpatched software or systems not properly secured. Employees might be lured into visiting infected Web sites or opening malicious e-mails. Malware then tried to take advantage of missteps in the system.

Jeff and Frank Renkin, Daryl's replacement at Red Zoya, had been housed in a Holiday Day Inn Express off nearby Water Street and were given an office on Wall Street in IT operations not far from the Exchange itself. Jeff was surprised the software development and computer operations were housed here, as it was some of the most expensive real estate on earth. The location was especially questionable, as the main data center was in New Jersey. The Exchange's primary IT operation could have been housed any-where; much of its supporting IT operation was, in fact, in Chicago. Appar-ently, NYSE Euronext had money to burn.

Access granted to a receptionist or data-entry employee was the weakest link of the Exchange's cyberdefense because through those users, malware could gain entry into the system. Receptionist-level accounts on the net-work position served as Red Zoya's starting point. Frank and Jeff were given contractor key cards to enter the building and assigned a shared office. They found it to be standard IT issue. Jeff had worked in dozens, likely more than a hundred, similar offices, each interchangeable with every other. The staff itself worked from cubicles, with managers occupying real offices around the perimeter. Jeff and Frank were given one of the small outer offices con-taining two desktop computers with flat-panel monitors, a modest gesture acknowledging the significance of their work but really chosen for privacy concerns.

The staff was told that the consultants were software contractors finish-ing the last stages of a project on-site. They were given computer accounts with the limited access permissions of basic staff unaffiliated with any par-ticular group or project. The e-mail program that came with the accounts contained a directory of users, while the browser was programmed by de-fault to open the Exchange's intranet portal. That page served as a central source of company news and was a hub to which department and team sites were linked. It also served as a search facility that enabled users to find docu-ments and sites across the network. With no more information than that, Jeff and Frank were to launch their attack.

Neither Jeff nor Frank had been surprised at being hired by the Exchange, or the nature of their project. NYSE Euronext was entirely computer and software driven. It was essential that the trading public and world financial system have faith in the Exchange's operation, so its security needed to be as close to perfect as possible.

There had always been problems with operationalizing high security. The keys to the Exchange were information and transaction speed. During the crash of 1929, the ticker tapes that recorded trades and were the lifeblood of traders had run hours behind events. The growing lag had spread panic and, it was believed, intensified the financial disaster. Traders had speculated in the dark, acting on rumors, many of which later proved unfounded. Reforms, including faster ticker machines and new regulations concerning trades, had improved transactions and renewed traders' faith in the Exchange but never eliminated a lingering level of unease.

NYSE Euronext traded equities, derivatives, futures, and options of nearly every sort. It listed nearly ten thousand individual items from more than sixty countries. The Exchange's markets represented a quarter of all world-wide equities trading and provided the most liquidity of any global exchange group, meaning it was almost always possible to actually make a trade. It was rapidly working to become the only exchange any trader would ever need for every kind of financial trading transaction.

As a consequence, NYSE Euronext had embarked on the greatest expansion in its history. When the expansion was completed, nearly all the world's trades would, at some point, pass through the Exchange's computers. The envisioned future was breathtaking in its audacity.

Nothing so innocuous as a bit of untargeted malware was going to bring the integrity of NYSE operation into question. The implications of broad distrust in its security were simply unimaginable, not just to the Exchange, but also to the interconnected world financial system. It was a system that operated largely on faith. Break that faith, and a financial catastrophe of epic proportions loomed.

As the pair had expected, NYSE system security was first rate. But once past the initial layer of defense, Jeff discovered the same erratic patching he had seen time and again with companies that asked the public to trust them with their private information. Some of this exposure had to do with time, as a certain delay was inherent in how patching was actually performed. First the vulnerability had to be detected, which usually took place only after an exploit that took advantage of it was released. It then took the software vendor, security research firms, or in-house shops anywhere from two to four weeks to develop mitigating configurations and a corrective patch, which would then be rolled out. The actual patching itself was time consuming and many times failed to receive the immediate IT attention it deserved, resulting in another delay until a patch was finally applied to the company's software, though too often even that failed to take place.

Part of the reason for delays and failures was simply human error and sloppiness. But there was more than just negligence involved. Every business had to make an assessment of the consequences that might arise from installing a patch. Updates were not always smooth and could create any number of unintended problems. Businesses, therefore, tended to err on the side of assuming the patch might compromise their software or interfere with something that interacted with it. In many cases, security risks were balanced against the risks to business processes, and then there was a period of reflection, during which the consequences were weighed. Sometimes after deliberation, the patch was intentionally never installed.

But whether holes were left unpatched as a result of a conscious decision or from plain ineptitude, they remained open doors for aggressors who might come later. Banks with household names too frequently had tin-box defenses within their outer walls, even though they usually adhered to industry-approved responses and followed cybersecurity best practices.

In the case at hand, an unpatched vulnerability in Payment Dynamo, a popular business application, was the missing brick in the wall that had separated Jeff and Frank from the fantastically complex internal IT network connecting the Exchange's hundreds of servers and thousands of employee PCs.

This was the first time Jeff and Frank had worked on-site together, and it was going well so far. Persuading Frank to join him at Red Zoya after Daryl's departure had not proved as difficult as Jeff initially feared. Though Daryl and Frank were old college friends, Jeff had known the man nearly as long. There'd been years when he had little contact with Frank, though they'd met in person to compare notes and complain from time to time when they worked with the CIA. Their work was related, often overlapping, and if colleagues didn't go around the bureaucracy occasionally, then nothing would get done.

For a time, the two men had been on the same Company league ball team, where Frank played a competent second base. He was of average height and a bit thin. Both on and off the field, he was even-tempered and solid. He approached everything methodically.

Frank had a background in technology, with a degree in computer science, and he'd joined the CIA after college. But instead of moving into computers, which were then in their relative infancy and not a priority, he worked as a field agent for seven years, employing his computer knowledge as a cover. Frank never spoke of his assignment much, but Jeff surmised that he'd been the real McCoy, trained in tradecraft. He'd been stationed in the United Kingdom and Spain, neither of them hot spots, and as a consequence spoke excellent Spanish.

But Frank gave all that up when he decided to marry Carol, and a safer and more predictable life became a priority. Theirs was a happy marriage, and the couple had three young children. One measure of Frank and Carol's close relationship with Daryl was that they had named their third and likely final child Daryl.

Frank had done well when assigned to Langley. He worked just two years as a cybersecurity researcher with the Company while obtaining a graduate degree before becoming a team manager and from there moved further into technical management.

At work, Frank's personality and appearance caused him to blend in, to be forgettable, which must have been an advantage, Jeff decided, when he'd been a case officer. For all that, he had no problem pulling his own weight or standing up to other managers in the relentless internecine struggles that marked CIA bureaucracy.

It had been the ongoing struggles for ownership of cybersecurity charters among various government organizations that finally wore Frank down. Once he became eligible for a pension, he was open to Jeff's offer. When he put in his papers, he'd been serving as the assistant director of Counter-Cyber Research.

More than once over the last eight months, Frank had mentioned to Jeff how little he missed the Company. The only part of his new job he disliked was the occasional travel assignments required of him. It might be a digital age, but some things still had to take place on-site. Direct access was especially common with highly secured companies. Though Jeff worked every day since arriving, Frank had squeezed in a weekend trip to his Maryland home.

Jeff's decision to remain on the job had been rewarded late yesterday morning, when the pair succeeded in positioning themselves for final penetration into the NYSE Euronext core operating system.

Frank had turned to Jeff with a profound smile and said, "That was as thrilling an achievement as I've ever experienced with computers. No wonder you love this job so much."

8

MITRI GROWTH CAPITAL
LINDELL BOULEVARD
ST. LOUIS, MISSOURI
10:54 A.M.

Jonathan Russo started over, trying to make sense of the incomprehensible. If his first pass was correct, the company was $16 million in the hole since the opening bell. Not only was that a great deal of money for Mitri Growth, but it also wasn't supposed to be possible. The firm had experienced temporary, unanticipated losses previously, but never anything like this.

In 2010, the NYSE Euronext opened its new trading hub in northern New Jersey, just across the line from New York State. Located at the site were the actual computing engines that formed the heart of the Exchange. The hub had been built to increase transfer speed, as most trades were now executed by computers rather than by individuals; to give transactions a greater measure of security, both physical and digital; and to increase profits.

Though rather ordinary looking as a building, the 400,000-square-foot data center was a contemporary fortress. There was but one way into the windowless structure, and that entrance was located not at the street address but in the rear. Surrounded by a river on one side and a moat about the rest, the trading hub was invulnerable even to a car bomb.

The visible building was an illusion, an outer wrapper that served much like medieval armor. Within it lay the actual structure. And while the hub's physical barriers were formidable, augmented by skilled armed guards and bomb-sniffing dogs, every electronic security measure possible was in place as well.

From this highly favorable location, the facility had ready access to any number of cybernetworks, along with two independent power grids. It also possessed its own backup electrical generator system. In fact, the facility had two of everything. An ever-increasing percentage of equities and options trading in North America was processed within its powerful servers. It was critical that it never fail to process them.

The facility was also designed to provide a colocation opportunity for trading firms seeking high-speed access to its engines. In an arrangement known as proximity hosting, the trader pods were each twenty thousand square feet and cost millions, not including the significant ongoing access fees. With the first pods selling out before the hub opened, construction was already under way to provide another five. These housed entire computer ecosystems used primarily by hedge funds and trading firms. The proximal location allowed clients to conduct trades in microseconds, and in this industry, being first meant everything.

The logic was simple: For every one thousand feet a hedge fund's servers were distant from the Exchange engines, one-millionth of a second was added to a trade, the length of time it took light to travel that distance. The NYSE servers processed more than one million orders every second. Each trade required the acquisition and processing of data, then a return of the decision. The process was accomplished in microseconds, round-trip. Colocation offered traders a highly profitable advantage, which explained why the pods leased for such exorbitant sums, a significant income stream for the Exchange.

The NYSE wasn't stopping with hub expansion. It was also feverishly constructing a series of microwave towers from Manhattan to its operation in Chicago, more than seven hundred miles distant. Microwave technology allowed the transmission of data in 4.13 milliseconds, 95 percent of the theoretical speed of light. The chain of towers would replace the existing fiber-optic cables, which transferred data at just 65 percent light speed. NASDAQ already had similar towers in place. NYSE's structures reduced latency by three milliseconds at a cost of $300 million, and were expected to be highly profitable.

Mitri Growth had acquired a proximity pod in New Jersey, though its trading code was written at the office here in St. Louis. One of the beauties of high-frequency trading was that it could be managed from anywhere on earth.

Russo glanced up at his team. They were feverishly at work to remedy the disaster still unfolding. Did he dare pull the plug? He was reluctant to do so before he knew what was taking place. But Mitri Growth couldn't sustain a loss like this for long. The hedge fund catered to high-end investors. In fact, much of its $250 million came from the personal portfolio of the company's Lebanese founder.

But if Russo's people could get this fixed before close of trading, there'd still be time to undo some or much of the loss. If the losses were real, that is. What he suspected, and what had thus far prevented him from acting, was the possibility of an aberration created by the new algo the team launched. The computers stated that Mitri Growth was losing money, but they might mistakenly be reporting a freakish reaction to the new software, not actual trades involving real money.

His chief assistant, Alexander Baker, had first proposed the possibility to Russo earlier in the day, when they discovered that the trouble came from the test code of the new program. His team was acting on the assumption that the test code had somehow activated in the production system, where it discerned the actual trades, but was reporting back to them using one of the fictitious scenarios embedded within it. The team was testing each of those in an attempt to confirm their hypothesis.

In the meanwhile, Russo's computer continued to claim that Mitri Growth was hemorrhaging capital. He looked at the wall clock with a sinking heart. If they were wrong, if this loss was real, they were running out of time to recover.

After eight years with Jump Trading in Chicago, Russo had joined Mitri Growth the previous year and assumed supervision of its ten-person programming team. He arrived right after the founder had taken the step of acquiring a proximity hosting pod at the NYSE Euronext hub.

Jump Trading was one of the earliest companies to migrate to electronic trading on the old New York Stock Exchange. Known for its cutting-edge algorithmic trading, the company had established itself as one of the founders of the new digital trading world.

With a Ph.D. in computational mathematics, Russo had worked in creating the algos, as they were commonly known, that generated the company's profits. He'd enjoyed the work, but in his view, too much of what he devised had been vetoed as too risky. Jump, he'd discovered, was too conservative for his taste. He couldn't understand the persistent aversion to a higher level of risk, which made possible far greater profits. He should have been a very wealthy man by now, rather than one with just a few million. The challenge, and profit sharing, Mitri Growth offered had been the career change he was searching for.

The founder of Mitri Growth wanted cutting-edge code to exploit the company's recent, expensively acquired proximity advantage, but more than that, he'd challenged Russo to discover new ways to leverage capital out of the Exchange. The assignment was entirely possible, and Russo was eager to discover the next clever means to achieve his mission. The best part had been the founder's willingness to run with Russo's instincts in crafting algos.

Traditionally, stock trading took place in a pit. Sellers stood there, offering stock at a certain price using hand gestures; buyers either bought or didn't. The price was constantly fluctuating in the pit, in sight of everyone. With the introduction of computers, all that had changed. Stocks were no longer bought and sold at a public location by traders. Now the work was done by machines. As late as 2005, 80 percent of all stock and equity trades were still executed at the New York Stock Exchange, but computers allowed those trades to complete not just more quickly but also remotely. The pit could be anywhere. The consequence was that by 2009, just 25 percent of all trades originated at the Exchange; the rest occurred within alternative trading systems known as ATSes.

That was the primary reason for creating the New Jersey hub, and for giving key traders such as Mitri Growth favored access. The Exchange needed this not just to stay profitable, but remain relevant as well. Already, similar Exchange hubs were opening or under construction around the world. Forty global "liquidity hubs," as the Exchange preferred to call them, were planned. A major hub in Basildon, east of London, was already operational and linked.

Despite public statements to the contrary, the key to all the NYSE expansion was the high-frequency trader, or HFT. Initially, computers had introduced greater efficiency into an aging system, but it wasn't long before the bright code writers known in the industry as "quants" began figuring out ways to take advantage of a computer's ability to process enormous amounts of information at inhuman speeds. Once they inserted the code authorizing a machine to buy and sell when specific conditions existed, without human interaction, it functioned like a moneymaking robot. High-frequency traders now accounted for most of the action reported on the Exchange.

As in sports competitions, when it came to high-frequency trading, speed made up for shortcomings. If one performed enough transactions fast enough, one didn't necessarily require the best code. Volume and speed compensated for minor missteps. Still, those with superior code, preferred access, and the most powerful engines made the most money.

At heart, HFTs were profitable because the computers knew the trading price of a stock anyplace in the world at the same instant and simultaneously compared it to the options price. Then, with lightning speed, they bought and sold on any detected difference before the Exchange's trading computers could adjust for price fluctuations. One of Russo's young designers had crafted an elegant bit of code that gave Mitri Growth the ability to predict the options price just ahead of its competitors, based on dozens of inputs and trends from across securities and exchanges. That was the algo they'd launched just after midnight with such high expectations.

The unspoken truth about HFTs was that they worked very much like a Las Vegas or Atlantic City casino, which takes a piece of all the action. It didn't matter to Mitri Growth if the market went up or down. It could ride a stock up, or short it on the way down. What counted was the action, because Mitri Growth's algos were structured to make money either way. It was not unusual for an HFT company with as few as thirty employees to earn a net profit of $1 billion. That was Mitri Growth's target with Russo's new algo program. But, as in a poker game that required a high stake to compete, money could be lost as quickly as it was won.

And that's what Russo was seeing—if the downturn was really happening.

Just then, Baker walked up. Tall and prematurely balding, his chief assistant had elected to trim his hair and grow a goatee to compensate. "Well?" Russo asked.

"We've ruled out the test code."

"So the new algo isn't performing in production the way it did in simulation."

"It doesn't seem to be." Before launching a new algorithm, Mitri Growth fed it current market data to see how it would have reacted in the past. Though not a perfect predictor of future success, it was the best validation the team could perform before letting a new version out to compete with everyone in the real world. Still, a slight unanticipated pattern and coded protections could cause the algo to become unstable in practice.

"So what's different now?" Russo asked.

The senior programmer shook his head. "We have no idea."

"So you're telling me these trades are real?"

"I'm afraid so." Baker cleared his throat. "We have to shut down, Jon. Then regroup. It's going to take days to figure this out and fix it."

"All right!" Russo snapped. "Take us off." He buried his face into his hands and slowly exhaled. He had to tell the founder. "How much?" he asked without looking at the screen, struggling to control himself.

"Twenty-three million. Hey, it could have been a lot worse."

9

From the day they started with this project, Jeff and Frank had enjoyed playing hacker. It was one of the more satisfying aspects of their job, especially when they succeeded. "This is the New York Stock Exchange," Frank had said when Jeff told him about the engagement in their D.C. office. "Do you think we can do it?"

"My bet is that we can. No matter how much a company depends on computers, no matter how big it is or how solid its reputation, its software and network are so complicated, the demands to make the process responsive to the market so great, that there are cracks everywhere. If we probe long enough, we'll get in."

"That's a little unsettling. This is a major cog in the world financial system we're talking about."

"Yes, it is."

They launched the pentest by casing the network from their low-privileged workstation. Jeff ran his own tools to develop a map of the systems in the network, looking to obtain as much information as possible from his position as an outsider. Once that step was completed, he ran other tools, attempting to connect to the systems at the ports used by standard system software and applications. He observed and carefully examined the responses he received. Even error codes returned when his attempts were refused revealed information, if nothing other than what software version was running, along with a few configuration details.

While Jeff was doing that, Frank trawled the Exchange's intranet directory, following links to the connected Web sites and scanning documents for tidbits of useful intelligence relating to the jump servers. He located a year-old document for the Universal Trading Platform, or UTP, which contained lists of names and user accounts for the team that deployed trading software to the New Jersey engines.

The UTP was designed to support all trading scenarios with submillisecond response time known as latency. The platform was integral to the Exchange's functionality and capable of being expanded as necessary. It also allowed outside parties "easy integration" within the NYSE Euronext global marketplace, which meant traders could pursue an endless variety of strategic initiatives of every type.

Frank was amazed at the lax approach to a system so essential to the world's financial security. He had anticipated that the system would be accessible only to NYSE Euronext's most trusted software engineers. Instead, many of the major traders had all but unfettered access. It was like a bank allowing its biggest customers to play around with its software to make things easy on themselves.

The consequence was that high-frequency traders typically tested new algos, live, on the Exchange, in secret. More than once, they were believed to have nearly caused a catastrophe. For one week, a mysterious computer program had placed orders, then canceled them before they were executed. Those algos made orders in twenty-five-millisecond bursts involving some five hundred stocks. In so doing, the program occupied 10 percent of the bandwidth allocated for the Exchange, certainly shutting out legitimate traders, just to test software in real time. That seemed to Jeff and Frank an unacceptable risk, but it was routinely permitted.

They'd conducted their reconnaissance exactly as a hacker would, constructing a schematic of the Exchange network. This included Web sites, server software, antivirus systems, user accounts, and their roles. Both of them noted potential points of vulnerability from time to time but this phase of their operation was primarily about collecting intelligence.

As they'd anticipated, the Exchange network was segmented into two zones. The first zone was standard issue to most companies and considered both insecure and untrustworthy. It constituted the public face of the Exchange, offering the usual applications anyone visiting a company on the

Internet expected to find. It was also where the workstations and servers supporting the business operations of the Exchange operated. The second zone, where the actual trading engine functioned, was buried within the interior of the site and locked down. For security reasons, it was not linked to the Internet.

The two zones were connected through dedicated computers called jump servers. Those servers substituted for the more traditional internal firewall. A jump server was designed to act as the secure conduit between the two zones. In other words, though anyone could access the public zone from their personal computing device, to enter the secure zone, one had to pass through a jump server, the sole gateway to the core systems.

One inherent advantage of the jump server was that all the tools required for network management were maintained within a single system. This made maintenance and updating a straightforward process, performed in a single location. Access permissions were tightly controlled, and all operations performed on it were continuously audited and monitored as well. And it could be thoroughly locked down.

But it was much like keeping all one's eggs in a single basket. This system had the advantage of isolating a vital gateway, which made it easier to control, but the disadvantage of presenting a single target for hackers to penetrate. If the jump server remained secure, it was a wall against intruders; if it failed, it served as a highway for them. It posed as their greatest challenge, but as a consequence, it was also their target.

Jeff's tool had identified servers in the Exchange running Payment Dynamo, and on the US-CERT Web site, he learned that a slew of security bugs had been recently patched with an update from the vendor, Payment Data Corp. The bugs were only the latest of a string of holes found over the last year in this particular package, a product that was not unique to the New York Stock Exchange; it was used for many applications within a wide range of financial institutions. For all that, neither Jeff nor Frank had been surprised at its poor design. They saw the same thing time and again. Like fancy chrome-plated door locks easily bypassed, this package offered no sophisticated security. The designers had focused on its utility, as what it did made the sale, not how well it was secured.

When the recent patches were released, FirstReact, the cybersecurity research firm that had reported the vulnerabilities, began selling exploit code for them at a hefty price. This practice, while controversial, was common. FirstReact specialized in discovering holes in software, as well as in writing exploits for those vulnerabilities and ones others had reported. Their customers were willing to pay a premium to gain protection against a hacker discovering the flaw and exploiting it.

Companies purchased these via subscriptions, ostensibly both to check for their exposure by trying the exploits out on their own networks, and develop and deploy mitigations specific to their environment. Because many of the vulnerabilities were unpatched when FirstReact sold them, they were "zero days," and could be used to spread malware and perform targeted attacks if they fell into the wrong hands. For that reason, FirstReact had a policy to sell them only to publicly traded companies and government agencies from a list of U.S.-friendly countries. But the assumption that knowledge of both the bugs and means to exploit them wouldn't leak was flawed. The fact was that some of the buyers, typically government agencies, used them to infiltrate foreign governments for espionage and to cyberattack criminal and terrorist organizations.

Jeff viewed zero day bugs to be the digital equivalent of nuclear weapons and believed the only way to make sure they didn't fall into the wrong hands was to strictly limit knowledge of them.

In this case, Payment Dynamo's vendor had released patches just a week earlier, so while the bugs weren't zero days, there was a chance that the Exchange hadn't yet rolled out the fix. So that it could stay competitive, Red Zoya was one of the companies that paid the FirstReact subscription fees, so Jeff was in possession of the exploit codes to match the vulnerabilities and had used them to break into the fourth Payment Dynamo server he tried them against.

That's where he and Frank had pried a space open yesterday.

10

Bill Stenton placed the telephone in its cradle and leaned back in his chair. This is happening too often, he thought. It was the third call in the last two weeks, each from a senior director on the Exchange, each with the same complaint. He'd been receiving similar calls for months.

His right hand had developed a tremor, and he placed his left on it. He closed his eyes for a moment and forced himself to breathe deeply, to slow down. Always tightly wound, he worked hard to present himself in the assured manner expected of someone in his position. He checked the clock on his computer screen. In three hours, he'd have his first double Scotch. He pulled his mind away from the thought.

Earlier, he'd received a call from a financial institution. The caller was a college fraternity brother who reported having experienced unanticipated and significant losses in a major trade. On such calls, Stenton had observed no pattern in the type of company or in the nature of the securities involved. In some cases they'd been hedge funds, in others private investment groups, in another a retirement fund—but in every case, the complaint was the same: Something out of the ordinary had taken place during a major transaction, which resulted in an unexplained reduction in the anticipated return, losses well outside the anticipated parameters.

The most common complaint was that HFT algorithms that had been reliable in the past, previously providing a profit within the margins established, were suddenly showing dramatic failures. As HFT systems were all located at the hub, they should have had the least latency. Instead, trades that should have netted a modest profit or at least been neutral ended up implausibly losing tens or hundreds of thousands. In more than one case, the loss had exceeded a million dollars.

Until now, Stenton had viewed the complaints, each taken in isolation, as so much griping by traders who were not keeping up with the game. Dealing with complaints like these came with the territory, but over the past few months, their rate and the magnitude of the individual issues had caused him to suspect there might be more to this than the usual Wall Street whining.

Still, Stenton had explained to the callers that it was not unusual for brokers to blame the system when they made a bad judgment call or when the market suddenly moved against a position they'd taken. In these days of high-speed transactions and high-frequency trades, that was to be expected. Yes, he understood that men and women had been fired, careers likely ruined over unforeseen moves, and that the losses had been significant enough to place the survival of some of the smaller financial institutions at risk. But the system wasn't at fault, Stenton was sure of that and had said as much. He told them he knew they wouldn't like it, but that was the reality.

But in the last few weeks, he'd also received two calls from other men he knew personally, reasonable brokers with serious questions about what was taking place. They'd been puzzled at unanticipated losses, not suspicious, and Stenton assured them that all was well with the Exchange.

But taken together, the string of calls caused him to rethink his position. He'd been searching for common links in the complaints. He thought perhaps there was a shared broker somewhere in the mix, or common stock. It might have been a time-of-day issue or the location of their programs in the hub. He had some of his top data analysts working to mine the available data, searching for any correlating factors.

Now Stenton held last week's report from the Chicago office. An IT operations manager there, Vince Piscopia, had forwarded a report to his superior, which then landed on Stenton's desk. As director of the Trading Platform IT Security for NYSE Euronext, he was in charge of this issue, but so far he wasn't certain how to respond. The day after receiving it, he'd copied the report to all his senior staff and his key analysts, requesting input.

What he didn't tell anyone, what he scarcely allowed *himself* to think, was that perhaps all these issues were connected.

What the IT manager in Chicago had reported was a file concealed within the core of their system, software outside the directory listing command. He'd been unable to access the file or determine what it did. What he'd been confident of was that it was not part of the legitimate function of the Exchange.

The IT manager, Piscopia, had speculated that it might be a bit of legacy code left over from one of the periodic updates of the system. Unnecessary code was left behind from time to time, but never before had it been hidden, and there was no way to know if it was harmless or somehow interfering with operations. In the same report, he stated that he'd also uncovered trades that were not properly registering and speculated that they were related to the code. This raised the same possibility in the mind of the Chicago IT manager as it had in Stenton's.

Impossible as he found it to accept, just maybe they'd been hacked.

Stenton shivered at the thought. He was at the helm. If the Exchange had been hacked and clients were experiencing losses as a consequence, his career was finished. In the worst-case scenario, one that in his fear he deemed possible, he might go to prison.

This possibility had come to his attention since Jeff Aiken had been hired and started his penetration test. Stenton had considered alerting the consultant but decided instead to see what Aiken and his man came up with on their own. Also, alerting them would leave a record of his suspicions, which so far existed only in his thoughts. It was his hope that Red Zoya not only stumbled onto what Chicago had described but also figured out what it was in the process. That was his safest course of action.

Just then, a tech poked his head into Stenton's doorway. "I'm Marc," he said. "You asked to see me?"

Stenton recalled that Marc Campos worked on the core trading platform team on one of the trading modules at the heart of the matching engines. There was no more sensitive operation in NYSE Euronext. He was one of the techs who attempted to trace a suspect trade a financial institution had reported to Stenton.

"Yes, come in. What do you have?"

Campos was over six feet tall, thirty-three years old, with dark skin and average looks, though his eyes bulged slightly. Originally from Portugal, he'd worked for the NYSE for the past five years, and his performance had been outstanding. He spoke near colloquial English with just the trace of his native accent. He was one of the handful of techs with unfettered access to the core of the Exchange's trading system. This was the first time Stenton had met with him alone though he'd seen Campos from time to time in staff meetings.

For several minutes, Campos described the steps he'd taken in tracing a reported $8.7 million loss in a transaction by one of the smaller financial institutions that had lodged a complaint. The referral had come directly to Stenton from a broker he'd known for years, a very reasonable man who was more perplexed than angry at what had taken place. When Campos finished, he smiled and made a dismissive gesture. "I worked on it until the trade just vanished. There was nothing I could do."

"Have you seen this before?" Stenton asked.

"Sure, but not often. Some of these offshore funds like to remain off the radar, you know? They don't like anyone knowing what they're doing. They go to great lengths to conceal their tracks beyond the minimum they need to trade with the Exchange. I've attempted to trace back trades with them, usually as a result of an SEC subpoena, and not always been successful, though you understand it's not really my area."

"Well, thank you anyway. I'd hoped for better news."

Campos hesitated, then said, "I've also been working on this Chicago report you sent out a few days ago."

"Any luck?"

Campos shook his head. "I don't see any sign of it. I think the guy in Chicago was confused somehow. He was likely misreading what he was seeing. Frankly, I don't see how anything could get into our system undetected. We're as locked down as you can get. Do we have his data? Maybe I'm missing something."

"No. I requested it, but he didn't come to work today," Stenton answered. Campos nodded in return and Stenton asked, "So for now, you don't think this stealth file exists?"

"I can't see it—" He paused and smiled. "—but then, it's supposed to be hidden."

Stenton thought a second, then took the plunge. "I know that you've been with this department for some time now, Marc. Do you think there might be a connection between the trade you traced and this hidden file Chicago reported?"

Campos looked surprised at the question. "That's an interesting idea, but there's nothing that connects them in theory. And there's no way a secret file could get into the engines. If by some magic it did, we'd be all over it in an instant. Like I said, I don't think this file even exists—and if it does, from what I read, there is no indication of what it does, if it does anything. Not only that, but we run an incredibly complex system. If getting an unauthorized file into the system is hard, manipulating a trade is simply impossible."

Stenton sighed. "You're right. I guess I'm just getting paranoid."

"Is this what those two are working on? Red Zoya?"

"Why do you ask?"

"The timing. I thought maybe you'd put a team on this even before the guy in Chicago made his report."

"No, that's something else." Stenton eyed Campos, then said, "Thanks for dropping by. I'll let your manager know I requested this meeting, so no concerns there. Have a good day."

"When you get the data from Chicago, you'll pass it along?" Campos asked as he stood up.

"Yes. Of course. We need to figure this out. And as for Red Zoya, just let them be. They aren't connected to this at all."

11

In practice, a trusted Exchange employee accessed the secure zone by first logging in to the jump server through an account specific to that zone. Since gaining their toehold in the system, Jeff and Frank were next tasked to compromise someone with privileged access.

Working from their office at IT Security that afternoon, Jeff and Frank had been consumed with analyzing the log-in records on the breached Payment Dynamo server. They soon identified a systems administrator who routinely connected to it from the other systems. When a user connected, the encrypted version of his password was cached by the server, allowing the user to connect to other servers without having to reenter the password. Being able to connect to different systems using a single entry of credentials is known as "single sign on" (SSO) and penetration testers, just like hackers, took advantage of SSO's caching behavior to execute what was known as a "pass the hash" (PTH) attack on other systems. This attack used the cached cryptographic hash of the password, a form of shorthand, to impersonate the user and connect to remote servers. Servers verified only the hash of passwords, not the passwords themselves. Because of the considerable security risk, systems administrators were never to use their administrator accounts when logging on to other servers remotely. Jeff knew it was a common practice, however, either because of ignorance or sheer laziness.

Within minutes, they'd successfully infected the administrator's computer. For now, they had administrative rights on the insecure network only, not the jump servers and therefore not the secure network they sought. But so far, they could view all the users in the network, identify their computers, even change their passwords and create new accounts, giving themselves administrative permission.

They were confident, however, operations of this kind were audited to prevent the kind of tampering they were doing. Automated software trolls checked logs and flagged unusual reports to detect illegitimate or unauthorized activity.

Next, Red Zoya targeted the team members from the UTP list Frank had identified. Working remotely from the administrator's own workstation, they determined the computers that corresponded to those users. Some users were inactive, but most were not. It was necessary to employ different users for different functions to prevent any security tool monitoring user activity from spotting the same user executing different operations at the same time. Frank and Jeff gave one account administrative permission to the computer of another user whom they believed had jump server access. Next they logged in to that user's computer, connected to the system of the programmer they were targeting, dropped their software backdoor, logged out, and then removed the administrative access to conceal their tracks. Even if part of their trail was spotted, it would be difficult for anyone to connect the dots.

During the next phase of their penetration attack, Jeff and Frank performed an enhanced reconnaissance on the UTP programmer's system. They were careful to keep their presence at a low profile, operating only when their user was logged in, so the activity blended in. They read his e-mail, the documents on his system, and observed the software environment, all undetected.

They finally ascertained the jump server system to which the user connected. The issue they now faced was that the jump server required a two-factor authentication, which meant that a password alone wasn't enough to get through it. When gaining access, the user read a pass code shown on a USB key fob, issued with a small LCD display on it. They then entered this number, along with a personally chosen four-digit PIN as the password. This scheme ensured that access required both possession of the USB key fob and knowledge of the PIN. And because the pass code changed every sixty seconds, it could not be saved and reused later. This meant that Frank and Jeff had to wait for the moment when the user logged in to the jump server, at which point they'd piggyback onto the connection.

They set up an alarm to notify them when the selected user was establishing his jump server connection, then resumed mapping more of the intranet systems and users. They created organizational charts, along with a thorough map of the network. This included the names and roles of users, names of servers and software installed on them, and the systems to which the users had access. They would submit this evidence with their report as proof they'd successfully penetrated the core of the trading engines and reinforce the picture of the damage they could have caused if they'd been genuine hackers.

During this phase they determined that the UTP system was running Linux and was locked down with "whitelisting," a security policy that allowed only software digitally signed with a special key that only specific users had access to. They would have to place their own software on the system in the secure zone, and for this it had to be signed so it would appear to be authentic. To this end, they monitored the e-mail of several users until they spotted a programmer who was about to submit an update package to the UTP system. They immediately planted their software, along with configuration information that caused it to connect out to their software on the jump server once it was deployed to the UTP system through him. In this way, it was taken as part of the legitimate package and was digitally signed by the NYSE Euronext signature along with the update and then installed on the UTP system.

Now they just needed their user to connect so that they could plant their software that would act as a bridge from the UTP system to the compromised Dynamo Payments software via the jump server. Only then would they be able to reach into the UTP system and remotely control the software they had just planted there, giving them unfettered access to the most important financial trading engine in the world. This would complete the entry they'd already begun.

The hours passed as they waited anxiously for the last piece in the puzzle to fall into place. They continued their mapping effort and documentation until their alarm alerted them that their primary user was connecting to the jump server.

"We're up," Jeff announced while not taking his eyes from the screen. Frank rushed to stand behind him, and they monitored the programmer's progress, then rode in with him without difficulty. They took no time at that moment for celebration, only exchanging a quick glance of elation. The minor crack they'd created was now an open door.

Once inside, they established their own connection, placing their software on the jump server, which connected it to the UTP system, completing the link and establishing remote control from their own system. Before exiting, they set up their second backdoor on the other side of the jump server, one that meant they could bypass this process in the future.

"That went smoothly," Frank said.

"I told you we were good."

12

Richard Iyers scanned the crowded bar and eyed a young woman at the far end. Blond and trim though a bit plain, with an oval-shaped face—and with that perpetual pout, just his type. She was laughing as she held her iPhone in front of her. From time to time, she took a quick look at a chubby man with a bright face, who was sitting at a table with two others not far away. They were playing a game, very likely one of the new ones on Toptical, currently the hottest social networking site. The man looked like a coworker, not a boyfriend.

Iyers checked his watch. There wasn't enough time. Well, he'd seen her here before and would see her again. Athletic, naturally slim, Iyers was an attractive man. His light hair was brushed across his forehead in a boyish cut. His eyes, however, were set just a bit too closely together. They and his mildly lanternlike jaw prevented him from being genuinely handsome.

He looked at the menu and considered ordering a cold beef sandwich. This might not be London, but the pub did a decent job with it. No, better later. Iyers took a sip of Double Diamond ale, then over the glass spotted Marc Campos weaving his way toward their table through the noisy happy hour crowd. The man's beer was waiting for him.

Campos scowled as he sat, his chin at an accusatory angle. He didn't touch the drink. "I think you're nuts," he said without a greeting.

Iyers grinned. "Maybe. I'm inclined to think the possibility is one of my assets."

Campos looked around, then leaned forward. "You're the one who made the coding mistake. I warned you about it at the time, and when you didn't act, I told you to fix the problem, not—" He hesitated, lowered his voice, then said, "—kill someone. I was talking about the file you left hanging out there."

"Dead men tell no tales."

"What's that supposed to be? Funny?"

"Not at all. It's a statement of fact, one you should appreciate, given your emphasis on security."

"You may very well have ruined the entire operation."

"I don't think so. No one's going to find anything."

"They don't know he's . . . gone for good yet, but he didn't report to work today. When he doesn't tomorrow, they'll check. Before long, people will be looking."

"So he took off." Iyers lowered his own voice, though with the surrounding noise there was no chance of being overheard. "They aren't going to find him. I weighted him with rocks and dropped him into a sinkhole just off the stream. It was all overgrown with vines and crap. He's fish food and gone for good."

"Maybe you were seen."

Iyers shook his head. "No chance. We were in a remote area. Relax. I was careful."

"Listen to me. This guy took yesterday off; you called in sick. Someone looking at this might wonder about the coincidence."

"You've got to be joking. I live in New York, this happened outside Chicago. There's no connection between the two of us. Anyway, I took the train. There's no record I ever left the city or that I was ever in Chicago."

Campos stared at Iyers, then said, "I hope you know what you're talking about. Because if they find him, who knows where the trail will lead."

Iyers shrugged. "Not to us. You worry too much, Marc. Anyway, he's a nerd. Nobody kills a nerd for writing code."

"When I sent you a copy of his report and told you to fix the problem, this isn't what I meant. You had to know that."

Iyers made a face. "Yeah, I understood, but the guy was closing in. He reviewed operational logs while looking at a software failure from last month.

You saw the report. He spotted that there'd been more than an acceptable number of connections between Vacation Homes and the trading engine. Automated security didn't spot it, but he had."

Iyers leaned forward. "Marc, he wasn't going to let it go. He'd spotted our file. He didn't know what it did yet, but he was working on it. I checked on this guy. He was tenacious and ambitious. Come on. There was nothing I could do that would have diverted him. In fact, if I'd changed anything in the software like you wanted, he'd have become suspicious that the culprit was someone who'd seen his report and was trying to cover his tracks. There aren't that many. We don't want anyone checking into what we've been doing this last year. There's a lot at stake. You've said so yourself. It's worth an extra risk or two." Iyers sipped his drink, then changed the subject. "How's Carnaval coming?"

Campos looked reluctant to move on. After a long pause, he said, "I think it will be ready for Toptical next week. There are still some bugs to work out."

"This will be our first IPO," Iyers said greedily. "If it goes smoothly, our take should spike dramatically. It's ideal for an expanded version of Vacation Homes."

"I agree, but no more mistakes. We'll be uploading the code soon. It must be seamless, understand?"

"I get it." Iyers looked aimlessly about the room, then said, "Did you find out about those two guys in the office?"

Campos, though, was still on subject number one. "Don't go off the reservation again. You hear me?"

"I hear you. What about them?"

"I'm serious. The next time you do, you'll have to answer for it." Campos leaned back in his chair, then drew a deep breath. "Stenton told me they have nothing to do with Vacation Homes."

"Do you believe him?"

Campos thought about that a moment. "I guess. I'm pretty sure we're not their target."

"I can't get them to talk about what they're up to. I've tried without being obvious. They're very closemouthed. I did a little online research on them. They both used to work for the CIA, did you know that?"

Campos briefly looked stunned. Then he lifted his drink and took a long swig.

"Jeff Aiken's the boss," Iyers continued. "It's his company. He's big in cybersecurity. He's rumored to have saved the world a couple of years ago." He smiled.

"What are you talking about?" Campos's thoughts were still on the idea these men worked for the CIA. He'd read once that no one ever really left the Company. The thought was sobering.

"Some kind of Internet terrorist attack. You remember all those incidents, the ship that ran aground in Japan, the near meltdown, some hospital deaths? They're supposed to have been caused by al-Qaeda. I read on some forum this Aiken guy blunted the attack. There've been other things too. A plane crash in Turkey."

"What? He's some kind of secret agent?"

"Nothing like that. Just really good at snooping around systems."

"Shit. Just what we need."

Iyers leaned even closer and spoke very quietly. "I can fix this too, you know."

Campos was startled. "Don't even think about it." He looked about again. The place was really getting crowded. "If more people . . . go missing, it's going to draw attention we don't need, especially with Carnaval coming online."

Iyers pursed his lips. "I can make it look like an accident."

"I said no, and I mean it."

"Ask your boss. I'll bet he sees it my way."

"My boss?" Campos pulled himself up. "What are you talking about?"

"You don't think I bought that line about this being your operation, do you? It's too slick, too big, and sometimes you don't make decisions right away. I'm just saying, check with your boss. Don't take this on yourself."

"Richard, when I came to you about this, I never said a word about violence. We write code. Vacation Homes is about making money. Nothing else."

Iyers stared at Campos, and then he took a drink to mask his thoughts. The guy's a fool.

Iyers was from Upstate New York. He possessed a congenial manner and had the knack of getting along with everyone while being close to no one. Since he formed his partnership with Campos, his self-image had taken on an unexpected aspect. He'd never seen himself as an outsider before, though if he were honest with himself, he always stood aside and looked in on normalcy. Those who played by the rules and lived conventional lives had always seemed to him to be suckers. Only when it came to women had he always felt himself to be a bit outside the norm, and even then, he wasn't entirely convinced his behavior was all that unusual. Men just didn't talk about it.

Then the economic meltdown had come, and with it a fresh appreciation of the worldwide financial system. He'd always stayed within his specialty, but now he studied the so-called system and saw it for what it was: an elaborate means for the corrupt to profit with the appearance of legality. That didn't surprise him so much as his failure to realize it sooner.

An infrastructure specialist at the Exchange, Iyers managed the deployment of software and the configuration of the NYSE Euronext data center systems. It was a position of extreme sensitivity. The systems included third-party software, such as antivirus and systems management software as well as internal software. He was also part of the team responsible for deploying much of the trading software that was the heart and soul of the Exchange.

He'd met Campos three years earlier, and within a few months, over beers in this very pub, Iyers shared his thoughts. A few weeks later, Campos met with him in private and laid out the scheme, presenting the operation as his own. The two men were ideally suited to make it happen, given their responsibilities.

"I estimate our personal take at ten million dollars each," said Campos on the night they closed the deal.

Iyers had nodded, his eyes flashing in greed. For an instant his mind had been filled with the thoughts of what he could do with that kind of money, the life he'd lead. Images danced before him, living rich in the Caribbean someplace, hosting parties full of hot girls. But the truth was, Campos already had him when he'd described the operation. This was his chance to hurt the Exchange, hurt it badly, to get back at the rich fat cats who thought they had it all figured out, a chance to make a statement.

And it was an opportunity to see just how far he could assert his power. He'd have done it just for that. The money made it an even better deal.

"You know," Iyers said, "there's talk about missing money."

"What talk?"

"Some of the big brokers are complaining about not making what they expected in trades. I've not heard anything official, just comments during breaks, but Stenton's getting nervous about it."

"Stenton's always nervous. That's why he drinks so much."

"He's a drinker?"

"You didn't know? Take a hard look at him on Mondays. You'll see. Anyway, if you can believe it, I was told to trace one of our own transactions."

Iyers found that amusing and chuckled. "How'd it go?"

"I was impressed. I did everything I'd normally do, and after two days, the trail finally just vanished into nonsense. I knew what we'd done, but from the side I was working on, I couldn't make anything out."

"See? We have nothing to worry about."

"I guess. But if our code gets identified and reverse engineered, they might trace it to one of us, no matter how clever we think we've been."

"I don't see how. We routed it through other users and servers that you and I don't have rights to. I used half a dozen laptops to set my part up and ditched each of them. There's absolutely no trail back to me."

"Let's hope so."

Iyers suppressed his immediate response. Instead he said, "So what did you tell Stenton?"

"Just what I told you."

"Did he believe you?"

Campos nodded. "Sure. Why not? I don't think I'm the only one he talked to about this, and no one had any luck, from what I heard. That's when I asked him about those two guys."

The men sat without comment; then Iyers said, "So what do we do? From what you say, we need to neutralize Aiken and Renkin. If you don't want me doing it the easy way, I'm open to suggestions, but I still think you need to take this to your boss."

"I don't have a boss. Just drop it."

"If you say so."

Neither spoke for some minutes. Iyers finished his drink and gestured at the waitress for two more. Campos looked deep in thought. The blonde at the bar laughed in triumph. The chubby guy at the table grimaced and set his phone down. The place was getting very noisy.

After the drinks arrived, Iyers said, "I haven't seen any real money yet." This was his recurring complaint. Campos had given him less than $100,000 so far.

"It's cooling off. I told you. We agreed."

Iyers shrugged. "I'm just saying." He looked around the room. "You know," he continued, "I have the feeling that time is running out on us, and a whole lot faster than you talked about. I haven't taken these chances for what little I've seen so far. Just so you know."

"You may be right about time. I'll get back to you on how we'll proceed." Iyers smirked but didn't say what he was thinking. After a long pause, Campos said, "Can you insert Carnaval without any bells going off?"

Iyers pursed his lips. "I don't know why not."

"No shortcuts."

"Enough of that. I told you at the time why I had to do it that way. There's nothing I can do about it now. If we make any changes at this point, they'll spot it and know for a fact something's up."

"Yeah. I get it." Campos picked up his second drink.

"I don't like these two guys working in the system," Iyers said.

"I don't either." Campos set his drink down and looked off to the side, still not answering the implied question. And in that gesture and silence, Iyers got the unstated message.

He grinned and extended his hand. He touched Campos's forearm in reassurance. "No problems, amigo. No problems. I'll take care of it."

DAY THREE
WEDNESDAY, SEPTEMBER 12

THE IPO HIGH-FREQUENCY TRADERS DESTROYED

Commentary
September 12, 11:30 A.M.

Palo Alto—Every IPO contains risk. It's an axiom of the stock market, yet time after time, financial experts behave as if each IPO is a guaranteed win for all concerned. For evidence of the inherent risk, you need look no further than the IPO for the well-regarded, high-frequency trader BATS Global Markets, Inc., in 2012.

No company appeared better prepared to launch an IPO. BATS was at the time the third-biggest U.S. stock exchange company and was a highly respected, innovative player in high-frequency trading. It was seeking an infusion of capital through its IPO to better compete with NASDAQ and the New York Stock Exchange. Since it ran its own exchange, it elected to handle the IPO itself. Everything was set for what was expected to be a highly profitable day. Instead, the stock opened just below the projected IPO price of sixteen dollars, and then continued falling as high-frequency traders came on board.

Within minutes of offering its stock, BATS announced it was having "system issues" with its own IPO. Ironically BATS stands for "better alternative trading system." To everyone's surprise, the company's software was unable to accurately display ticker symbols for a wide range of stocks. Then a single trade for just 100 Apple shares executed by BATS drove the stock down more than 9 percent. The Apple stock quickly recovered, but confidence in the ability of BATS to handle trades did not.

A high-profile public offering by such a well-known company draws keen media and public interest. Yet too often in recent years there have been significant problems with them. These problems have often been complex and buried within the vast software used to control the offering. As a consequence, what went wrong is often never adequately identified or fully grasped.

These new trading problems are the product of computers, and while computing power has increased efficiency and profits, it has also brought with it new issues that are still not entirely comprehended. The reality is that no one really understands the complex software. All major companies now have board-level risk committees charged with assessing what is taking place and alerting the company to what it needs to do. Yet time and again, the measures taken to prevent the problem BATS experienced have, upon examination, been found to have caused them, or at the least have proved inadequate in stopping them. The consequence has been the notorious Flash Crash and serious glitches in the Facebook IPO.

BATS had been an expert at IPOs, and yet it fell victim to its own bad software and predatory HFTs that sold the stock short once their algos sniffed blood. Its stock fell to pennies by the time the company abandoned the IPO, which was immediately deemed the worst of all time. BATS has announced no date for its next attempt.

HFTs tend to lurk offshore. No one knows how many there are or how vast their holdings. Their ability to manipulate the market is coming under increased scrutiny. In some instances, their motives have even been questioned, as it is not clear who controls them.

But for now, BATS remains the first IPO killed by HFTs.

FOR MORE INFORMATION, VISIT LESLIEWASHINGTON-TONE.COM

International PC Review

13

Victor Bandeira climbed into his taxi helicopter, gave Sergio, the pilot, a nod, and then sat back in his comfortable seat. Almost at once, the blades whirred and the agile craft lifted from the helipad atop the towering building. Sergio was one of the old guard, a foot soldier and bodyguard he'd relied on for years. He'd had him trained to serve as his pilot, not wanting to rely on outsiders.

Bandeira adjusted his charcoal gray Armani suit and checked his watch. Though he adhered to the Latin custom of tardiness, especially when it was he who had called the meeting, he did not take it to extremes.

The city skyline was spiked with gleaming glass towers, symbols of the new Brazil and its regional economic dominance. After five centuries, the nation was at last assuming a significant place in the world. Brazil had always been the land of destiny, filled with promise and expectation but falling short time and again, sinking into a morass of corruption and failure.

There'd been frenzied eras of economic boom before, first made possible by sugar, later by coca, then by rubber. Each had brought enormous wealth into the country and made a handful of families very rich. But this boom-and-bust cycle, always dictated by circumstances outside the country, had never solidified into sustained growth or elevated Brazil to world power status.

Now all that was changing. Over recent decades, the government had instituted initiatives to give the economy greater balance, and with the development of a vast oil reserve just off the coast, a measure of sustained prosperity at last seemed possible. Bandeira was not a patriot, but all these changes meant opportunity, and if nothing else, he considered himself a man who knew opportunity when he saw it.

He took in the smog-shrouded skyline as the helicopter weaved its way among the towers. He counted a dozen other air taxis exactly like his own. At any time, there were as many as five hundred of them plying the busy skies over this city of twenty million. He looked through the brown blanket of smog beneath to the traffic-clogged streets even farther below. More than six million cars were crammed into those congested streets. He'd be two hours getting to his meeting down there. In the air, the trip took less than ten minutes. So it was that the rich and influential moved about São Paulo, flying above the masses like demigods.

But convenience and efficiency weren't the only reasons for the sky taxis. The sky was safer than taking the streets. Kidnapping was a cottage industry in the largest and richest South American city. More than one acquaintance and countless others Bandeira knew by reputation, men who had taken great measures to ensure their safety, had been seized off the street and held for ransom. If the kidnappers misjudged and asked for too much, if the family or business moved too slowly, or sometimes just to make an early point, an ear of the victim was hacked off and mailed.

So common was the loss of an ear among the rich that more than one local surgeon specialized in its reconstruction, extracting naturally formed cartilage from within the victim's body and from it creating a replacement. True, the new one was hard and unyielding but it looked like the real thing even on close examination. The daughter of one of his colleagues wore such an ear while two young men of his employ took another approach, proudly displaying the space where the ear had been shorn, testament that they'd been taken and survived the ordeal.

One of Bandeira's rare failures had been in his effort to control the local kidnapping trade. In his view, it was out of hand, targeting those it should not, giving the city a reputation for violence and danger that was not good for business. Bandeira had long planned to bring kidnappings under the control of his gang, Nosso Lugar, "Our Place," or NL as it was known. But the other gangs, *quadrilhas*, engaged in kidnapping were too disorganized, too impulsive to be brought in hand. They viewed Bandeira with the same distrust with which they saw the official authorities.

After several futile efforts, Bandeira had called a halt to his attempt—for now. He'd concluded that consolidating the gangs and bringing them under his control was possible only through a sustained violent effort. These thugs understood death. The consequence was that a significant number of them would have to be killed. The other approach was to kidnap members of their families, cut off a few ears, make demands. Only then would they begin to see the light.

Bandeira had discussed this approach over lunch with the regional police and military commanders, two men with whom he'd worked for decades. The three of them had talked it through at length, and they'd agreed it could be done. And they were prepared to let Bandeira do it, providing cover as needed. If one gang was preying on another, it was possible that the media would accept it as a positive outcome and for once divert attention from law enforcement's own failure. But both men had cautioned that only a sustained campaign of terror and violence could succeed. In the end, the gangs would have to be brought to heel. These were vicious men who lived violent lives, so nothing less than absolute dominance would work. A half effort would only bring on a war of greater ferocity, which they did not want.

"What we need," the city chief of police had said through his cigar smoke, "is a period of civil unrest. A time of street demonstrations, assassinations, vendettas, and murders to serve as cover for your operation. Who would know? And when all was over, you'd be in control."

The general smiled. "This is Brazil. We all know such a time is inevitable. If I were you, I'd plan accordingly. You can count on us," he'd said reassuringly.

So the plan was in place. The police and army fed information to NL every week, and one of Bandeira's trusted captains kept the plan updated with names and addresses. When the time came, Bandeira's organization would act. The consequence would be an end to random kidnappings and the return of greater safety to the streets. Targeted kidnappings would become the norm, quiet ones that would still be lucrative. The wealthy of the city could breathe a little easier, and foreign investment would not be so timid.

Bandeira contemplated the numerous ways he'd profit with a sense of satisfaction. The helicopter banked, righted, then began a gentle approach toward the round landing pad atop the gleaming Banco do Novo Brasil building. Bankers, Bandeira thought as he mentally reviewed that morning's agenda, they should all be shot.

14

Now that Jeff and Frank had penetrated the NYSE engines and had free access to the core of the trading processes, they were in the final phase of their engagement. They continued employing the specialized tools that Jeff had devised over the years and which he guarded closely. They were the key to what he did and made his work not only less tedious but also more effective. The hardest part of the decision in hiring an outsider, even a friend like Frank, was granting access to these jewels.

He had other tools, which he made commonly available at his presentations in order to spread his brand and facilitate better computer security. They were accordingly closely identified with his name and that of his company.

At this point, the pair was mapping the extent of their success while also searching for other ways and paths to more deeply penetrate the system's cyberdefenses. Having succeeded at their primary task, they took a more leisurely pace now, less intense. The pentest was essentially complete; what they did now was icing on the cake.

Jeff could simply have informed Stenton of their success, but he had a reputation for going a step further and typically did something harmless to the system that persuaded even the most dubious company executive that he'd accomplished what he said he had. He reviewed things he'd done in the past, wanting to pull something clever and distinctive from his bag of tricks. He decided to ask Frank for ideas.

Taking an early lunch, they'd stretched their legs and walked up to Chinatown. After selecting a restaurant at random, they sat in as quiet a corner as was possible in Manhattan at midmorning.

"You know," Frank said, eyeing his pair of chopsticks dubiously, "we haven't been spotted yet. At first I kept thinking an alarm's going to go off, but instead we've got the run of the place. I understand why the antivirus programs don't know we're there, since we aren't in their database, but their other automated security programs ought to be spotting our presence. They continuously monitor operation commands and functions. If any company in the world understands how to mine data looking for the smallest hint of something unusual, it would be the Exchange—at least that's what I thought."

"So far, we've only planted a bit of code, and that looks legitimate. All we've really done is take a look." Jeff smiled. "And we've been clever."

Frank split the chopsticks apart, then tested them in his right hand. "They don't know we're there, so we can set up all the offshore accounts we want and move money into them. Of course, it would leave a trail, since computers are keeping tabs on the money, but there'd be nothing to stop us. The trick is leaving nothing behind that points to us personally, then whipsawing the money around the world until it's impossible to trace."

"Do you really think that's possible in this day and age? It seems to me that every digital transaction can be traced."

"In theory, sure, but if you're clever about it, create a host of dead ends to mask the money trails, then bury all of them in complexity, you can slow such a search to a crawl. In practice, you can make it never ending. It would take a dedicated team and time, but it can be done. We saw terror groups doing that with the money they raised and stole all the time when I was with the Company. We did sometimes catch it, but we knew what we found was just the tip of the iceberg. The Internet, Jeff, is as close to infinite as anything on Earth. You don't have to block anyone trying to trace you, even if it were possible; using robo code, you just have to keep stretching the trail ad infinitum. It works out to the same thing."

"Maybe. Better, though, if the Exchange never knew the money was taken in the first place."

Frank pursed his lips. "Yes, but how do you do that?"

"Maybe take it directly from clients' accounts, a bit here, a bit there, keeping in mind that a 'bit' in this case is a few hundred thousand, maybe a million at a time. Take a penny of every dollar out of transactions, for example. They might not even notice, and even if a client sees the loss, the Exchange doesn't."

"But if enough of them complain, the Exchange will get on it."

"You conceal the loss within their trading patterns so it doesn't look as if it's an Exchange issue. You know bureaucrats, always looking to avoid problems if they can. If you aren't greedy, all you're doing is skimming a bit of the cream each time. It might raise a few eyebrows, but there's no reason—in theory, at least—to cause any serious research. I think that's the better way to do it. Then you can bury it with electronic false trails like you say. And it's really only a variation of what the high-frequency traders are already doing, especially those hiding offshore."

"Good thing we're honest." Frank jabbed at his rice with chopsticks. He finally put them down and picked up a fork. "You know," he said, "I'm thinking about moving my nest egg out of stocks."

"Why's that?"

"I don't like a lot of what I've seen, but it's these high-frequency traders that really get me."

"What about them?"

"I don't care if a company finds a way to buy and sell faster. Paying for close physical access isn't fair, but those with money always have an edge like that. The problem with high-frequency traders is their manipulation of the financial system. And because they're allowed to hide what they do, no one really knows the extent of the manipulation."

"I didn't know you were such an expert."

"I'm not, but I'm getting there. Actually, I'm reading a book about it. It's really eye opening."

"You're obviously not working hard enough if you have time to read a book."

"It's part of research. A vital part, from what I'm seeing."

The problem, Jeff and Frank had realized from the beginning, was that understanding in detail how the Exchange worked was extraordinarily complicated. The professionals making their fortunes from Wall Street employed their own jargon, in part to convey ideas effectively but also to safeguard their propriety access to the lucrative trading system. Once stripped of the needless complexity, the system wasn't that incomprehensible.

"Buy low, sell high" was still the lifeblood of trading. Computers and their role in the international market had caused that basic rule to become more complicated than ever, but it remained the essence of the Exchange. When someone wanted to sell, they offered the stock at a specific price. When someone wanted to buy, they listed the price they were willing to pay. Between them was a difference. When one party moved, the transaction took place, not physically off to the side of the trading pit as had occurred at one time, but with nearly unimaginable speed.

Algorithms zipped through the Exchange's computers, searching for deals within the parameters the programmers had established. When a trade that fulfilled the parameters was found, it was made faster than the blink of an eye, with no human interaction.

The essence of this had always been to stand at the front of the line because there were always more buyers for deals at the right price than there were sellers. The logic was simple enough: More buyers at the listed price drove the price up. The stock available at a desirable price was gone before all the buyers were satisfied. Since getting to the front of the line was essential, the Exchange had a rule—the first to offer to buy was placed ahead of those to follow.

As there was more than one exchange in the world, stocks could be offered for sale or to buy at different prices at the same time. But like water seeking its own level, given time, every stock had but one price. The opportunity came when a delay existed in settling on that common price. In a process known as arbitrage, computers networked around the world reported differences in prices, and algos exploited discrepancies the instant they were discovered. HFTs made money if the difference was an increase in price, and most of them made money by short selling—that is, making money if the price fell. The difference was exploitable either way.

Those opportunities had always existed, but now with computers, they were hunted down as never before, and the chain of transactions took place at unbelievable speeds. This was the red meat for high-frequency traders and as a consequence accounted for a substantial majority of all trading activity, a percentage that grew with each passing month.

HFTs designed and unleashed more sophisticated programs than other trading systems. They paid for proximity to the Exchange's hub engines to get themselves to the head of the line, beating out more remote competitors. They also possessed a comprehensive understanding of the market's microstructure. No other traders understood exactly how the trading engines worked, precisely how trades were executed, how orders were prioritized—but HTFs did.

"I don't know," Frank said as they finished their meal. "It just seems to me that the stock market doesn't work any longer, not in any logical way. It's so complex and fragmented, no one's got a clear understanding of how it functions. It doesn't even seem to be about providing a marketplace where people can buy and sell securities. There's all this other stuff going on all the time. It's all smoke and mirrors, altered reality, like a video game. What's scary is that I don't think anyone understands all the new rules or the full extent and implications of this permissiveness. There used to be just a few kinds of trades and only a couple of places to make them. Now there are more than one hundred types of trades, and if you add the variations, it's well over that. And there are plenty of places where you can execute them. It's all intentionally complicated, if you ask me."

"It's computers," Jeff said. "They're a curse and blessing. They make high-frequency trading possible. And the billions of dollars they're taking all comes out of the pockets of pension funds, 401(k)s, and regular investors."

"It's worse than you think. As far as I'm concerned, these HFTs simply manipulate the market, like I said. Consider this: In an old-fashioned traditional physical trade, a man with a bag of money might stand behind the buyer, demonstrating his interest in buying even more stock if it became available. He never needed to actually bid on the stock to influence the price; simply existing was enough. His presence alone tended to drive up the price. It worked the other way as well.

"These HFTs have perfected a system in which they can appear to be that guy with the big bag of money ready to buy, *but without ever actually executing an order.* The consequence is that the sale or buy price moves, and once it moves in its favor, the HFT programs execute in a millisecond and make a profit. All the while, no one knows if the guy with the big bag of money even exists. In most cases, the HFT never owns the stock it is offering to sell. If things don't move the way they want—if the difference they spotted disappears before their order is filled—they just cancel it. As a consequence, over half the volume of orders processed by the Exchange are canceled. It's nothing less than tampering. They aren't making a legitimate offer to buy, or sell. They are trying to move the price to a point where they can make money. And nothing stands still. The HFTs are constantly inventing new, profitable ways to exploit financial transactions, novel ways only the sophistication—and speed—of their servers make possible.

"Listen to this," Frank continued. "In May 2010, the financial markets plunged into free fall with no warning. In just minutes, the Dow plummeted almost one thousand points, something like nine percent of its value. It was the biggest single-day drop in history. Nearly one trillion dollars disappeared into digital vapor."

"If you say so. I must have read about it."

"We all did, and if you're like me, it didn't mean a thing at the time. Some shares fell in value to a single penny, if you can imagine, only to rebound to, say, thirty-five dollars within seconds. And in high-frequency trading, 'seconds' is a very long time. It worked both ways. Apple, for one, briefly traded at a hundred thousand dollars a share—can you believe it?—up from around two hundred fifty. It wasn't alone. Then, within minutes, the stock market righted itself and recovered its losses.

"Trades were taking place so fast, a delay of thirty-six seconds crept into the system. Now, that's a lifetime in this world. What it meant was that what the computers, even the real traders, were seeing was half a minute away from reality, so they were acting based on dated data. It was like 1929 all over again. They bought and sold, thinking the price was going one way, when actually, it was moving the opposite direction.

"The collapse was so extreme, so profound, it was like watching a pedestrian being struck by a speeding car. Then, as you tried to deal with the horror of what you've just witnessed, the victim stood up, brushed himself off, and walked away as if nothing had happened.

"Traders were shocked at what they'd experienced. Everyone wondered if it would start again. But it didn't. They decided it was an anomaly, so they went back to business as usual right after. The SEC, *Wall Street Journal*, hedge funds, all looked for an explanation without success. All they did was give it a name—Flash Crash.

"Now, nothing like this could happen before computers, and that's the point. Traders seeing such fluctuations in prices remotely approaching these would have used common sense and not participated. They'd stand down. But the computers applied the logic of their algos and reacted instantaneously, without consideration of the consequences or logic of the situation. Stop and think about this for a minute. If a thirty-five-dollar stock fell to, say, two cents, would you sell? Would you even be taking part in what is clearly a bizarre phenomenon? Of course not. You have common sense, you know something is very wrong. But the computers don't think; they act. They sell at two cents, they buy at two cents, *if* there's money to be made. Reality has nothing to do with their world.

"There was a lot of unease, even though the market recovered. They'd seen the pedestrian walk away, but it gave them no comfort. Everybody was really nervous, and the lack of an explanation only made it worse. There was the suspicion, the near certain belief, that high-frequency trading was behind it all. About a half year later, the Security Exchange Commission's report was finally released. Just one enormous trade had gone terribly wrong, it said. That's it. And get this, the financial markets weren't prepared for it! That vulnerability, the SEC said, was because of the aggressive selling by HFTs whose computers had responded automatically to the market's illogical behavior, exactly as traders had suspected. You get a few HFT algos responding to each other's movements, and things spiral out of control before anyone realizes what's going on. It's not humans trading with each other; it's computers. Cross-market arbitrageurs, looking to score a quick profit, piled on and drove prices down something like three percent.

"What the HFTs did was issue nonexecutable orders in batches. These were intended to detect early trends or to test latency. Critics claim their purpose was also to clog the exchanges, to create noise, to outmaneuver competitors. Pretty cynical.

"Now, stay with me here. You have responsible high-frequency traders. Their algos are set to pull out when they see erratic behavior. But you also have irresponsible high-frequency traders who are not so smart. So what happened was the smart HFTs left the trading field to the dumb ones. That's why you had such crazy trading decisions.

"Here's the big part, in my opinion. All this was caused by a trade of just over four billion dollars on a day in which the volume was two hundred billion. Think about it. What would a larger trade do if it went awry? Four billion's a lot, but even more is not out of reach. What if the algos causing the disaster failed to correct themselves? What if the exaggerated prices remained fixed for more than a few seconds? And remember, these guys have all been forewarned now. They aren't likely to be so patient next time. The Exchange keeps telling everyone they've put a stop to these computer issues, but there's no confidence any longer in the integrity of the system. The same thing happened on the Shanghai Composite not much later. It collapsed six percent in just two minutes.

"The SEC report said that the regs that were supposed to prevent the Flash Crash didn't. And that the Exchange was still vulnerable to large and immediate transactions. Those involved in the financial markets decided that the Exchange understood a little of *what* had taken place but not *why*. They figured it could happen again, and it did."

"When?"

"Facebook and the disastrous BATS IPOs. Now the Facebook IPO was handled by NASDAQ while BATS did its own, but the lessons cut across the industry. Both of them had significant trading anomalies. What's going on is that there's a lot of unease and distrust in the worldwide financial community. The big guys have made plans against the day the next Flash Crash happens. The dark side is that if the immediate rebound fails to materialize, it would then be every man for himself. That's an eventuality these new algos have already been programmed for. The market won't have more than a few minutes to right itself before it's everyone acting in his own interest and to hell with the market. No one can predict the extent of the potential financial abyss."

"You're saying Thunderdome?" Jeff asked.

"Why not?" Frank said. "The worldwide financial system is so connected, and becoming even more so, why not? It's all run by computers, and even after such events, there were no significant security changes." Frank looked around the room. "Everyone's too busy making money," he mused.

"Not everyone. Plenty are losing it. So what's your plan? Bury gold in the backyard?" Jeff asked.

"That's just it. What do you do? The point is not to stay in the stock market, but if you stay in currency, with the way it's being devalued, you lose worth. So you buy property, right? Well, good luck with that. We've all seen how that goes. Getting the money out of the country and into a basket of currencies might work if there weren't so many regulations working against it, and at my level, it's not worth the effort. The point of all this is the average guy is getting screwed."

"So what else is new?" Jeff asked.

15

Following his meeting that morning, Victor Bandeira took the helicopter for the short ride to his residence in exclusive Macatuba. The small helicopter swept over the manicured estates below, banked left, slowed, then eased onto the helipad marked by two concentric circles and an X. The craft touched gently down and the pilot immediately killed the engine, then set the rotor brake. A minute later, Bandeira stepped out and walked briskly toward the main house, carrying a thin briefcase.

His son, Pedro, was waiting at the entrance, as the two of them were to have their midday meal here at Bandeira's estate. Afterwards, the young man would join his mother at her home across the city before returning to Rio. It was his twenty-fifth birthday.

Set on nearly twenty-five acres with a main house of some nine thousand square feet, the estate was a necessary extravagance, as far as Bandeira was concerned. To be perceived as rich was as important as to be rich. In many circles, this display was unnecessary, as Bandeira's position was well known, but he did important business, especially with foreigners, who needed to see his wealth on display.

The furniture in every room was specially built for the house. There were eight bedrooms, office space, a huge family room, and a dining room nearly as large. There was a four-season porch and terrace, a spring-fed pool, a game room he never used but his son enjoyed, as well as extensive grounds with fully mature trees and an orchard. There was also a guest and a maid's house, even an acre of native forest that served as a bird sanctuary. Through it and the grounds wound a creek. Altogether, it was enough to impress even the heads of state.

Pedro Miguel Ademar Bandeira-Carvalho was a handsome young man with sleek black hair and a slim body. He possessed a slightly bookish demeanor enhanced by the rimless glasses he wore. He was dressed casually, and on the streets of São Paulo, he would be taken for exactly what he was—an IT professional, given to long nights writing code.

By design, there were no visible signs of security. The estate had the latest in technology, but Bandeira relied primarily on a devoted team of bodyguards, whom he treated and paid well. They were discreetly located about the grounds, nearly all out of sight.

The operatives were under the direction of Jorge César. Tall, slender, mustached, and nearly always dressed in an austere black suit, he was utterly devoted to the elder Bandeira. The two had attended school together. Afterwards, César joined the police. When Bandeira assumed control of the cartel, César left law enforcement and became his full-time chief of security. A quiet man by nature, he blended easily into the background, always alert, in regular contact with his security team.

Father and son embraced, Pedro kissing his father lightly on both cheeks. Bandeira set his briefcase down, then took his place at the head of the long dining table. Pedro sat to his immediate right. Except for the servant who brought each dish, they dined alone.

"Here," Bandeira said, removing a nearly square wrapped box from his suit pocket. "For your birthday, my son."

Pedro accepted the gift with a smile, then unwrapped it as Bandeira watched his face keenly. When the young man opened the box to see the dazzling wristwatch inside, he grinned broadly. It was the latest Louis Moinet. "It's too expensive. Something more modest would have been enough. Really."

Bandeira pushed the box and wrapping aside. "I saw you looking at mine one day. I thought you might like one just like it. There's an engraving."

Pedro lifted the watch and tilted it so he could read the inscription: *Para o meu filho, Pedro, de seu pai amoroso.* "To my son, Pedro, from his loving father." He slipped the watch on, his grin never easing. Bandeira sat back, satisfied. He'd read the boy's interest correctly.

"Now, let us enjoy our meal."

They ate while discussing Pedro's work in Rio, Bandeira nodding in approval, asking an occasional question but not as he might at a meeting. This was a festive event, a time he'd looked forward to for several weeks. Anyway, he was well briefed on what his son did, in every aspect of his life.

When they'd exhausted the mundane topics, Bandeira asked, "Is Carnaval ready?"

Pedro nodded lightly, his mouth full of food. When he finished chewing, he said, "Nearly. I think we'll hit the benchmark."

"I'm thinking about upping the take with it."

"We've been on this for months now, *pai*, and we're only a few days out from the IPO. Changes at this date could create unintended problems if we don't have enough time to run a full range of tests."

"I understand. But you have a good team. And . . . I have pressing needs. You understand."

The pair waited as espresso was served with a dessert.

"We can try," Pedro said, "but I'm worried there isn't enough time." Bandeira nodded without comment. The men took a bite, and then, to change the subject, Pedro said, "You know, you always said that someday you'd tell me more about your life. There is a great deal I know nothing about."

Bandeira looked at him. "You would find it boring, I'm sure."

"I never met my grandparents."

Bandeira thought. "My parents? I suppose you are right. You're a man now. Actually, except for the family story, you surely know it all as it is." He leaned back and lifted a cigar from the table where the server had placed it with dessert. As he clipped the tip and lighted it, he said, "Where to begin? It was . . . so very long ago."

Victorio Manuel da Silva-Bandeira had been born in the favelas of Rio de Janeiro. As he told the story now, he slowly lapsed into his childhood accent, the patois of the poor and disenfranchised of Rio. He did it without thinking and realized it had occurred only when he saw the sober expression on his son's face. To speak the truth, Bandeira thought, I must speak in the language of truth.

His father, Miguel, had come from the north, he said, seeking opportunity in Brazil's premier city. He'd found a job as an automobile mechanic, worked hard, married late, and had just two children, Victor and a younger daughter, Maria.

"My mother, your grandmother," Bandeira said, "ran a cart that served meals on the street. You know the kind. You see them in every poor area of Brazil. Maria and I helped her from the time we were toddlers, but my father had greater aspirations for me and insisted I attend school when I was of age. He said I was smart."

Bandeira was just as smart as his parents had thought, and he excelled in school. They encouraged him and at some sacrifice found a way to pay for his clothes and tuition. When Bandeira was a teenager, his intellect and personable manner were recognized, and under a new government initiative, he received a scholarship to an elite boarding school. The program was designed to identify bright youth and give them advantages that would ultimately contribute to Brazil's emergence as a world economic power.

"Life was not easy on my parents," Bandeira said. "A new gang took control of the street where my mother set up her cart each day, and they demanded so high a payment, it was nearly impossible for her to earn any money. When my father met with the *chefe* and respectfully explained the situation, he was savagely beaten." Bandeira stopped at the memory, at the rage he'd known when he first saw his father's wounds. "Unable to go to work, he lost his job, and for a time my family's situation was very bad. I wanted to drop out of school to work, but he forbade it."

"What happened?" Pedro asked.

"My mother agreed to sell more than food from her cart. She had no choice in the matter, frankly. It was either sell the small, folded-paper packets or go hungry. When my father was healthy again, he returned to the *chefe*, knowing another beating might well result. He explained that his wife could not openly deal in drugs. It would drive away her regular customers and inevitably lead either to her arrest by police or death at the hands of a rival gang. He suggested instead that she serve as a lookout and from time to time as a transfer point for wholesale packages. She'd serve a better role for them this way.

"The leader apparently admired his courage, or saw the logic, because he agreed. My father found work with another garage and life went on. For a time. You will find this hard to believe, but I was one of the first at school to show a real interest in computers. I was fascinated by them, even wrote a bit of code. Don't ask. I don't have it any longer, and I'd never show it to you if I did. Because of my interest in computers and because of my background, I had many problems at school at first. Most of the students were from well-to-do families, and it was impossible to hide my own poverty. I worked hard on my diction, but it was several years before I rid myself of my accent. I was taunted and teased until I beat one of the older and much bigger tormentors. I threatened to do the same to any student who told on me. Thereafter,

I was left alone." Bandeira paused to reflect. "In the end, it was my ability as an athlete that led to my acceptance."

"So you were good at *futebol*?"

"Did you doubt it? I had more reason than most to work hard. It was important to me, more important than to players with greater ability." Bandeira talked about the school, the teachers, the course of study, the girls who attended their own school down the street. "They were like angels for us to worship from afar.

"When I was sixteen years old, everything changed. The situation on the street corner occupied by your grandmother had continued for three years with no real trouble. The family had a bit of savings. My parents did not tell me what my mother was up to, but Maria did. There was nothing I could do about it, and what other choice was there? Other girls I'd known growing up now worked as prostitutes; most of the boys I'd played with as a child were either drug dealers or thieves, or both—if they weren't dead or in prison. A few had taken honest jobs, but they lived no better than anyone else.

"A new gang wanted the territory. To make their point, they killed a number of the lookouts, including my mother and Maria. She was just fourteen. They'd simply been gunned down at the start of the violence."

Bandeira stopped. His face became soft as he said, "You'd have liked your aunt. She was delicate. When you smile, it reminds me very much of her. It breaks my heart sometimes." He sighed. "They gave me a week off from school to attend the funerals and mourn. I told my father that I was not going back, and he slapped me for the first time. 'You will go back, Victorio,' he said. 'You will succeed. Why do you think your mother worked on those streets? For what? Some beans and rice in her belly? It was for you, for you. You were her hope. We need no drug dealers in this family, no thieves. You were, you are, our salvation. Study, work hard, succeed.' That is what he said to me.

"So I went back to school and worked even harder. Three months later, my father was killed crossing a busy street. I never knew if it was an accident or if he'd said the wrong thing to the wrong man. That is when my life took a change I could not imagine. A few weeks later, I was invited to spend the Easter vacation with the family of my best school friend, Luís. He was a little wild and didn't study, but he wasn't a snob like the others. They lived here in São Paulo, and for the first time, I experienced up close the world of the rich." Bandeira gestured lightly with his cigar. "This world."

Ademar Carvalho, Luís's father, he said, was the leader of a local crime cartel. Though uncultured, he'd become very rich and had sought the appearance of legitimacy later in life. He lived in an exclusive gated community near the Pinheiros district of São Paulo. Carvalho was a hearty, robust man who doted on his youngest son. For two years, he'd been hearing about Bandeira—the tough from the favelas, star *futebol* striker—and then he learned of the deaths of his parents.

"'My home is yours,' he told me. 'You must enjoy yourself while you are with us.' That was more easily said than done. The boarding school had always seemed luxurious to me, with its peaceful central garden and clean solid rooms, the buildings on tree-shaded and safe streets. We students were well taken care of, and I'd always found the food abundant, even sumptuous. But this was a different matter. Afterwards, Luís had to persuade me time and again to join him until finally I became more comfortable with the servants and the Carvalhos' extended family.

"Ademar Carvalho had steadily worked his way up through the ranks of Nosso Lugar, emerging as leader some ten years before. His was not the largest such organization in the city, but it was well established within its area, selling the usual, running numbers, and providing women to the back-alley brothels."

Carvalho had been impressed with the young Bandeira. He knew the boy's background and systematically set about recruiting him. The most recurring difficulty Carvalho had was not rival gangs or the authorities; it was finding hardworking, loyal young men. Eighteen months after that first visit, when Bandeira graduated, Carvalho suggested he work with him a bit before deciding on his future.

By this time, Bandeira was ready. He'd paid attention, even asked a few discreet questions at school, read newspapers, gone to the library for more research, and understood just who Luís's father was. His own father, he'd decided, had been wrong. And because of that error, the street and gangs had taken his *pai*, his mother, and his sister away. There was no place for honest people in the world, definitely not in Brazil. Carvalho was showing him the way, and Bandeira intended to follow.

"And I've never changed my mind in that regard, Pedro. I have pursued the correct course for my life."

He'd worked a year in São Paulo, never on the inside of the operation but never left on his own on the deadly streets. He ran errands, delivered messages, supervised lower-level operations when the usual manager wasn't available. He was forbidden to possess drugs or a weapon himself. He was scrupulously kept away from all violence. The *chefe* had bigger plans for him.

As a reward for his good behavior, Bandeira was given access to the better brothels, enjoying them almost daily, and was provided with enough money to dress properly and to move in the more respectable circles when he wasn't working. After the year was up, Carvalho had taken him to lunch at his exclusive club.

"'I want you to attend the university,' he said to me. 'Luís refuses. I hope you will try to persuade him to join you.' In fact, by this time I rarely saw Luís. After school, he'd joined Nosso Lugar with a vengeance. He ignored every effort made to keep him away from the areas I was also forbidden. Rumor had it, he'd already killed two men, and he was never without a gun. Fast women, fast cars, cocaine were his stock-in-trade. I told his father I would try but—" Bandeira shrugged. "—he understood. 'There is much we do that is very addictive for the wrong kind. You can never be sure how men will react when given some power and exposed to what is out there. Luís breaks my heart. Do your best,' he told me."

It was agreed that Bandeira would take a degree in finance and business. Carvalho would pay for everything. When it was time, he would join the NL in junior management and begin his career. It went well for Bandeira, though Luís was dead within a year. Thereafter, Carvalho drew him even closer to him and his family, finally suggesting the marriage to his daughter, Esmeralda.

Lunch with Pedro had gone well, Bandeira thought as he set off for the city. Rather than be shocked by the story his father had told, by the harsh accent of his youth, his son had been intrigued, perhaps even impressed. No, it went better than he had feared. Relief swept over Bandeira, and only then did he realize how much he'd worried about telling him the story.

The young man seemed to have completely recovered from his anger at his parents' divorce six years before. Bandeira scowled at the thought. His former wife, Esmeralda, had not been suitable for his new station in life, not that it was her fault. They'd married young, and it was a good match at the time. Unfortunately, her approach to the bedroom had been traditional. Despite the reputation of Brazilian women as lovers, wives of the old school viewed sex as a service. Their attitude drove men to other women, but that was the way it had always been.

For the first years, Bandeira's only real disappointment was that they'd had just a single child, a son, at least. But in time, with his greater success as he'd moved in better and better circles, the uncultured and ever heftier Esmeralda became an embarrassment. Then she'd fixated on his many lovers and, to his surprise, began making demands. After that, he brought the charade to an end. These were modern times. There was no reason for him to be shackled to someone unsuitable, certainly not after the death of his father-in-law.

Still, the divorce had angered Pedro, and for a long year he'd refused to have anything to do with his father. That had hurt, hurt far more than Bandeira would ever admit. A Brazilian's son was as much a part of the father as he was his own person. The wound had gone deep, and Bandeira feared the estrangement would be lasting.

He'd placed his son in charge of the Rio team, responsible for an operation ideally suited for Pedro's attention to detail and technical background. Casas de Férias, "Vacation Homes," it was called. All Pedro had to do was keep on top of things and lead. And so far, the boy had done just that. He'd taken to his work with zeal, and Bandeira decided that his son might yet become a true man, a man capable of taking over the cartel when Bandeira's time was done. Not that that would happen anytime soon. He had years to go yet.

Curiously, it was Esmeralda who'd made this possible. Once she became his ex-wife, their relationship had suddenly improved, to his great surprise. She'd taken to dressing in the traditional black of a Brazilian widow, and he understood that within her circle of intimates, she spoke of him in the past tense, as if he were dead. At first he'd been shocked, and he'd confided in Carlos Lopes de Almeida one night over drinks.

"She is traditional, Victor, that is all," Almeida said. "She cannot accept divorce. It is not in her makeup. She has been married, she has a son, and now she has no husband, so she must be a widow. It is no more complicated than that."

Victor realized at once that he was right. As a consequence, he saw Esmeralda only alone, never around her friends, so she could maintain her façade—not that he had occasion to see her that often. Still, her name had been on many corporate documents, and it was necessary from time to time to obtain her signature. It was on such an occasion that she'd raised the subject of their son.

"I have spoken with Pedro," she said as they sat in her garden some months after the divorce. As a youth, Esmeralda had closely resembled the

Mexican actress Katy Jurado. That had been no small measure of her appeal, he'd come to realize. Now, forty pounds and twenty-six years later, the resemblance was impossible to find. She did carry herself with dignity, but that was an affectation of her putative widowhood.

"I have told him that the past is the past," she said, "that you are his father, and he must not treat you as he has." She paused.

"*Obrigado*," he said. Thank you.

Esmeralda inclined her head. "He has promised and I believe him. Call him. He will see you."

That was the moment Bandeira wondered at the prudence of his divorce. Other times such as this flashed in his memory, times when she'd shown wisdom and a greater understanding of life than he often possessed. She'd never condemned his career and he rarely spoke of it in her presence, but there had been occasions when she'd known of his troubles and each time given considered advice, advice he followed. Maybe he'd been wrong to shut her out of his affairs so completely all those years; maybe he'd been wrong to divorce her when he should have embraced her fully as a trusted confidante.

But it was too late for that. "*Obrigado*," he repeated.

"If I may suggest," she continued tentatively, "you should find a place for him in your organization. A place of significance, though I understand you must craft him carefully; he is still young and untested. But he has ability, he is willing, and . . . he is your son."

"I will do that." And so he had. Vacation Homes had gone well, better than he expected, but his computer expert, Abílio Ramos, had much to do with that. Ramos had brought his wide-ranging Internet gambling enterprises under control, and Bandeira had enormous faith in his ability. Still, there was no question that Pedro had found his place. One of the reasons for their lunch had been to give Bandeira still another opportunity to consider the young man's future. How long should he remain where he was? Where should he be moved next? Was it time?

When a longtime friend asked if Bandeira planned to change the name of the *Esmeralda*, he had shaken his head, saying it was bad luck to alter the name of a boat. The friend had accepted that, but Bandeira concealed the real reason.

Gratitude. Esmeralda had given him back his son.

16

That morning, Jeff had employed one of his Linux tools to perform a thorough inventory of the UTP system. After lunch, Jeff and Frank returned to their temporary office and logged on to the command and control, or C2, server to check the status of the automated scans of the UTP servers they'd left running. Jeff sat up straight. "Look at this. Rotorooter says there's a file hidden with a rootkit."

Rotorooter, as he had named it, was one of the programs Jeff routinely ran whenever he gained access to a system. It was designed to look for signs of rootkits, which were programs that hid files or other programs from the standard administrative and diagnostic applications a systems administrator would run.

"There shouldn't be anything hidden in this system, not where we are," Frank said. "Are you sure Rotorooter isn't giving you an FP?" Wonderful as Jeff's tools were, they did provide false positives from time to time.

"No, not entirely, but I don't think there's any reason it would." Jeff showed Frank the Rotorooter's output, and for the next hour, the men worked in conjunction, finally establishing that there was no problem with the tool, that a concealed file existed within the UTP, a place where none should. One odd turn occurred when Frank determined that embedded in it was the NYSE Euronext digital authenticating signature. With that knowledge they made several attempts to access the file employing standard system commands, all without success.

"Maybe it's something left from the original coding," Frank suggested, "something inadvertently squirreled away."

"That's possible, I suppose, but why a rootkit? Could Stenton have planted it as a test to see if we'd find it?"

"You mean as part of the pentest?"

"Maybe." Jeff paused, racking his brain for explanations. "Or what if it's some final security cloak to protect the trading software from an attacker who gets this far? Of course, the scans haven't found anything else hidden, and if this is a security measure, there should be others, wouldn't you think?"

"It could be the most security-sensitive file in the entire system, that's why it's been singled out for special treatment."

There was another long pause; then Jeff said with a low voice, "Or maybe it's malware." This was the most logical explanation, as rootkits were a tool of hackers.

"But it's got the Exchange's code signing signature."

"So why's it hiding itself?" Jeff countered. "Besides, the stuff we planted has the same signature. Whoever put it here could have used the same trick we did."

"Or it's someone in-house. That's more likely. It would make affixing the signature really easy."

Just then, the door to their office opened. "Ready for a break?"

Jeff looked up. Richard Iyers was standing there with a warm smile. His office was not far away. From the first, he'd taken Jeff and Frank under his wing, showing them about the building, answering questions but never intruding on their work. He had said he understood what they were doing was confidential. He'd even made his gym available, but neither had had the time to take him up on his offer.

"Not now. We're just back from lunch, and we've got a lot more to do yet today."

"All work, no play. Maybe tomorrow," Iyers said as he stepped away, careful to close the door behind him.

17

The long meeting broke, and the mid-level managers who'd attended filed out while top management lingered, as was often the case these days. Scattered before them were the electric-blue covers of the revised IPO prospectus just released by their principal underwriter, Morgan Stanley.

Brian Cameron, CEO and cofounder of Toptical, looked down at his iPhone as if he had no interest in continuing the meeting. Samantha Mason, known as Sam, sat opposite him across the expanse of the conference table. In the hallway, staff went about their business paying no attention to them behind the clear glass wall. The topic was the same as always these last months.

Money.

Molly Riskin had launched into her favorite topic with her usual animation, hands slashing the air, her brow moving up and down as she argued against the pending IPO. Chubby, with bitten nails, she was one of the company's first employees and had worked with Brian at his previous start-up, Enerva. She was senior VP of Toptical Sales and Marketing.

Gordon Chan, CFO, was to her left, while Adam Stallings sat opposite her. Dark, hard to work with on occasion, and a software engineer, Brian had moved Adam into management, a decision Sam thought was a mistake. He lacked the temperament, though she understood Brian's recurring dilemma. He needed people he knew in positions of responsibility, and he required people who understood the system. What it meant was that Toptical was being managed essentially by self-taught executives while the crucial software was being largely written by newcomers. That didn't bother Sam all that much, considering what the so-called professionals were doing to companies that had been household names during her childhood. As for the code, that was another story altogether.

The money talk was ironic in Sam's view as Toptical had all started out as nothing more than fun and games. She couldn't believe how fast a late-night brainstorming session had become tangible, how quickly Toptical itself had become a household name. She'd heard stories of the success of other "overnight" companies, many of them companies the general public didn't know, but this! Now they were a week away from becoming rich. Very rich.

"The IPO is set, Molly," Gordon said. He was a handsome man, fit with a finely featured face and near constant smile. "We heard you on this last year, and you've made your position clear many times since then. The decision is made. We can't cancel at this late date. You need to move on."

"Of *course* we can cancel," she said emphatically. "It's happened before. I'm not saying it will be easy and not cost us *some* money, but we've got it. If we stay as we are, then we remain in control, we can keep Toptical what we want it to be. Once we go public, we *lose* control. Doesn't anyone else see that?"

Brian glanced up. "The decision is final, Molly." He looked back down.

Molly stared at him as if he'd just walked into the room, blinking rapidly. "Okay, then consider this. The stock is *overpriced*." This was a theme she'd repeated for the last month. "We're set to go the way of Facebook."

"Nothing wrong with that," Gordon answered with a smirk. "Zuckerberg made out like a bandit."

"Sure, and so did a lot of those at the top," Molly continued, "along with the early backers and underwriters, but look what people *think* of them. They came across as greedy. I don't know about you, but that's not how I want to be seen. That's not *why* I work here. That's not who we are."

Sam eyed Brian evenly. He was fixed on his iPhone, which lay on the blue-bound prospectus in front of him, occasionally punching at it. She'd been living with Brian four years earlier, when they'd been bitten with the bug. She and Brian had seen the inherent weakness of Facebook and of the other social networking sites, anticipated how quickly users would become disenchanted as marketers leveraged them, and they stopped being fun. They'd constructed Toptical with all that in mind, more for the

challenge of it than for anything else. They'd thrown into the hopper everything they wanted in a social networking site, and a real company had
quickly emerged from that.

What they devised was a one-stop shop, enabling businesses and users to
establish accounts that integrated user groups, topics, family and friend
groups, affiliations, video, and much more. It was far more comprehensive
than Facebook because it had topics that served as discussion areas, a place to
post videos, pictures, and articles, buy media content, play interactive games,
obtain notices of discounts and coupons, and much more. It was of particular
use to business customers because it integrated their various public faces, but
let them connect to their personal identities, keeping the activities and
membership of each side linked, but still separate. From an investor point of
view it had a built-in monetization process, underdeveloped as yet, but dem-
onstrated the potential for a dramatic upside. The buzz surrounding the IPO
was everywhere.

Inevitably, the concept wasn't so original now as it had been then. Now
it seemed every major Internet player wanted in on the action. But they'd
been first, they were by far the biggest, and they had the brand.

"Who cares what people think about us?" Gordon said, looking around
the table for confirmation. No one reacted.

"We should," Molly insisted. "Right now, we're cool, like Facebook used
to be. If we stop being seen as cool, it will hurt us. It will affect how successful the company is down the road. We need to *think* about that."

"That's crap," Brian said, glancing up from the table. "You brought up
Facebook yourself, and it's doing just fine. What counts is the quality of our
product. Anyway, the time is right for this. We need to take adv—"

"We've got maybe a two-year lead on the others," Adam said. "That's
more than a lifetime in this industry. I think Molly's got a point. I'd like us
to keep control without having to consider investors, the SEC, all of that,
but I agree that this may be our only shot at real money. I get that, so I'm
on-board for the IPO. What I don't like is Morgan Stanley releasing more
shares. I think we're oversubscribed, and it's going to dilute our share value."

"They told me demand requires it," Gordon said a bit defensively.

"And what if their principal clients don't come in as strong as they claim?"
Molly asked. "What if demand isn't as high as they tell us it is? We've got
trouble that's what. The stock could go into free fall."

"The company's valued at a hundred billion dollars today," Brian said,
now fully engaged. "That leaves a lot of room for market adjustments."

"That's hype," Molly said. "It's thirty billion tops, Brian, like the prospectus says. The other figure is for PR."

Brian smiled mischievously. "It's still a lot of bil—"

"And where's the money coming from?" Adam said, interrupting again. "Isn't that the big issue here? It's not my side of the business, but the underwriters are concerned." He tapped the blue folder in front of him. "They dress it up, but it's there. It's why they released this at the last minute. They're covering their asses."

"Google, Microsoft, Twitter, even Facebook, they're breathing down our necks wanting to buy us out, and they've got *deep* pockets," Molly said. "The money they'd spend acquiring us would be a loss leader for them. They don't need to make money with us. We do."

"It's not just them," Adam added. "Right this minute, in some garage, there's another Brian and Sam working on an idea to take us out."

"What do *you* think, Sam?" Molly asked, looking at her eagerly.

Sam shrugged. "You all know what I think. I've said it often enough, and I was outvoted. You were one of those votes, Molly, if you recall. We should position ourselves for a takeover rather than risk an IPO. I agree with canceling next week. This prospectus gives us plenty of reason. Our subscribers will think we're rock stars. Our future is brighter if we're taken under the wing of a major player. We can cut our own deal, which leaves us running the show. We still get rich, but we get to keep control."

"She's got a point," Adam said. "Those two at Google want us so bad they upped their offer just last week. They'll cover any costs of canceling the offering. I ran the numbers for myself over the weekend. I'll do about as good with them as with an optimistic reading of the IPO. I could go with Sam on this, especially after reading this update."

"There's no risk," Gordon said, his eyes still fixed on Sam.

"Right. No risk," she said. "As for the IPO I agree the stock's overpriced. I don't claim to understand what our underwriters are telling us, but they've got us valued at one hundred times last year's profits. I think that's at least double where we ought to be. It concerns me." She tapped the folder. "This revised prospectus is a warning, Brian." She looked across the table at her former lover. This company had destroyed their personal relationship, and over this last year, he'd largely stopped listening to her. "What if Morgan Stanley's major clients back off like Molly says? I think this report is telling them to do just that. What's going to happen is that the public who love us and come in on launch day are probably going to take a bath, and Molly's right there too; it will hurt us. And we're vulnerable right now."

"We'll be rich," Gordon said slowly, as if speaking to children. He hadn't been there at the beginning. He'd come later. Brian had never told her why he'd hired him, but Gordon had joined a running company, and so he had a different perspective. He'd located this building for them for one. A former synagogue, it had been in a sad state of disrepair and never brought up to speed. Because of the poor heating and an inconvenient layout, everybody hated working in it, but he'd told Brian it was some kind of deal they had to take. It had an attractive appearance and impressed the second round of investors who were impressed by cool. It served as a persuasive forum from which he smooth-talked private investors, even handled some of the media duties. He was a natural.

And Sam trusted him about as far as she could throw him.

"Our early investors want their payday," Gordon said. "We need to get that. They're tired of us, tired of HDTVs in the work spaces, tired of our frat boy mentality, the lack of a dress code or even basic professional behavior." He'd argued against all of that since coming on board, Sam had to give him that. "They want a professional management team."

Brian made a face but didn't speak.

"The IPO's being *manipulated*, Brian," Molly argued, leaning forward aggressively across the table. "Wall Street doesn't care about Toptical, about our *vision*, how it changes lives, what it means to the world. All that matters to them is how much money the launch makes. And there are jackals out there who will sell us short at the first hiccup next week. We need to back out, *now*."

"I've got confidence in our underwriters," Brian said. "I'm not pretending I understand all the ins and outs. That's Gordon's area, but he tells me the price is about right. This isn't science, Molly. No one knows the real value of the company." With that last comment he shot a look at Sam.

Sam could still see what had drawn her to him: his smooth style, his steadiness under pressure, but for the last year, ever since the IPO date had been picked, she had this feeling that he was out of his depth, and knew it.

"Molly," Gordon said, "you're going to be very rich even if the underwriters are wrong. The initial shares being offered largely come from this table, and projections are that they'll be snatched up. It really doesn't matter to us personally what happens downstream. By ten o'clock Wednesday morning, we'll be more concerned about the tax bite than the price of the stock."

"That's something else we need to consider," Adam said. "Founders and early backers typically represent about ten percent of the stock first sold to the public. We're over forty percent, not as bad as Facebook was, but bad enough. It makes it look like we don't have any faith in Toptical and want to get our money while we still can."

No one spoke; then Brian said, "We're always one bad move away from insolvency. I think you all need to remember that."

"Thank you, Jeff Bezos," Molly said. "I'm not in this just to make money. Toptical *means* something. It changes lives."

"It's social networking," Gordon said, spreading his hands before him. "That's all. And what do you propose we do, Adam?"

Adam shook his head. "I don't know. Be careful I guess. Maybe do what Sam suggests. It's a lot safer."

Brian leaned back. "Look at it this way: We're top dog right now, and I plan to make sure we stay there." His eyes turned to Sam's face, as if acknowledging her role. "But the big boys are right behind us, not to mention the kids in the garage. We have no way of knowing if we can stay in front. We need to make it now. All this—" He gestured toward their building as if they owned it, as if everyone at this table loved it. "—could be gone in months if the public turns somewhere else. Frankly, I wouldn't want to be in Facebook's shoes right now."

"And what's this about changing lives?" Gordon said sarcastically. "Toptical takes people out of their boring existence. If they had real lives, they wouldn't be using a computer as their primary way to connect with other people."

Sam grimaced. "What if it goes wrong?" she asked. Brian looked at her sharply. "What if these wonderful underwriters are stacking the deck so they do okay no matter what? What if the IPO is a disaster?"

"That can't happen," Brian said evenly.

"It happened to BATS, and it was their area of expertise. Nobody made any money there. All they got was a black eye they'll never recover from. It can happen to us. Don't kid yourself."

Sam noticed from the corner of her eye that they'd drawn a crowd. She hadn't realized how loud they'd become. Several employees were gawking openly at them. Seeing her look they hurried off. Life in a fishbowl, she thought savagely.

"Let's settle down and focus on what we should really be concerned about," Adam said. "All that pricing stuff is out of our control. It's all in place now. It's the technology that really concerns me. I talked to someone with IT at the Exchange. They're using a new program for us. I don't like being a test subject."

"I know about that," Brian said. "It's a special program just for IPOs. They don't want any of the problems BATS had—or Facebook, for that matter." NASDAQ had courted Facebook to handle their lucrative IPO; then their software delayed selling for half an hour on launch day. It had sent a shiver through the market. There was no telling how much money it ended up costing the company because of lost confidence.

"Adam's got a point," Sam said. "We all know the track record of untested code when it goes public the first time."

"It'll be fine, they learned from their mistakes," Gordon said.

"What the hell do you know about it?" Molly snapped. "Stop pretending you know everything. You're the *finance* officer!"

They continued for another ten minutes and in the end, settled nothing. As everyone filed out Sam held Molly back. When they were alone, Sam said, "I know you're concerned. I appreciate the passion, but this thing is set now, Molly. I've had to come to terms with it, and so should you. We're just along for the ride at this point."

"I know. I know." Molly was close to tears. "It'll just break my heart if it goes bad. Toptical means *everything* to me."

18

Bandeira's office was located on the forty-third floor of the Edifício República, and he never failed to take in the expansive view at least once each workday. The towering skyscrapers, the choked streets below, even the ever-present pollution all represented wealth and power. They reminded him of just how far he'd risen. And as often happened at such moments, his thoughts turned to the past.

Though Victor Bandeira's rise within the NL had been greatly facilitated by his marriage to Esmeralda, Carvalho's unexpected death from a presumed heart attack just three years later placed him in a precarious position. Bandeira had not by that time been designated as the heir apparent—though that, it turned out, was what saved his life. He'd not been seen as a threat among those who vied for leadership.

Still, there'd been changes. For one, Bandeira had been removed from his safe sinecure and assigned responsibility for a street gang. The new *chefe* told everyone except Bandeira that the young man was soft, that he'd been coddled by Carvalho. To his surprise, Bandeira found he took pleasure in working the streets, taking part in the action, overseeing the executions or doing them himself. He understood finally the addiction of the streets, the allure of power, the sense of invulnerability that came with guns and violence.

But Bandeira was not a foolish man, and he knew that there was nothing in the streets in the end for him but death or prison. So when the opportunity came, after he'd proved his manhood to the *chefe*'s satisfaction, he was moved into finance, a safe cubbyhole where he was content to bide his time.

His movement up the ranks thereafter had been slow but steady. He'd been careful to remain on favorable terms with every potential leader and made no enemies. It had not been easy, but he'd managed to walk the tightrope. Only when he was finally in upper management, a mere rung or two away from the prize, had he acted. It had taken two deaths, one staged as an automobile accident, the other as a botched surgical procedure, but two years earlier, he'd emerged as the undisputed leader of Nosso Lugar. He'd moved quickly thereafter to clean out upper management of any potential rival. He'd not mentioned any of this to his son.

Over the years, Bandeira had studied the organization's cash flow and slowly became convinced that it should move away from activities that made them the target of other cartels. They weren't big enough to take them on. As *chefe*, he kept with the tried and true. NL still sold drugs within its territory and trafficked in prostitutes; these were the standards of their business, but he was careful not to expand. He ordered that they stop dealing in guns as he wanted to see fewer weapons on the streets and whenever he spoke with the other *chefes*, he made the point with them. Their men would always have the weapons they needed but it made no sense to be selling firearms to uncontrollable gangsters. He saw no sign that he was convincing anyone, but he kept at it.

Bandeira also cut back on the protection money NL took from small businesses. It no longer constituted a major source of income, and he knew from his own experience how counterproductive it was. He wanted thriving shops and stands in his area and his agents were able to use the loyalty of the merchants in other ways, as lookouts, to stash illicit items for a few hours or days, or to provide places of refuge when needed. In Bandeira's view it had all worked out for the better.

While working in finance, even before becoming *chefe*, he'd become convinced that the future of real money was in computers and the Internet. He'd followed closely the growth of cyber-crime and even before he'd become head man he'd set up operations. As a consequence, NL was a major world player in Internet gambling, running the three largest such operations.

He'd moved aggressively against his competition in the early days. He'd sent men to infiltrate other operations and sabotaged their sites at every opportunity. He'd used denial-of-service attacks against rival gambling Web sites and to that end had a team of bright young men led by Abílio Ramos setting up botnets constantly, botnets that sat idle for long periods until his other teams put them to good use.

A botnet was a collection of computers connected to the Internet, thousands of them, in which the cyberdefenses had been breached, and they'd been placed under the control of an outside party, unknown to whoever owned or operated each computer. The computers were co-opted when someone using them executed a bit of malicious software. They may have been lured into making a download, or been penetrated by a vulnerability in their Web browser, or even tricked into running a Trojan horse program, which likely came through an e-mail attachment, often from a known source. Such infected computers were used to recruit other computers. Once within the computer, the malware placed the computer under the control of the botnet's operator, known as the "herder."

Typically the herder directed the botnet group to his own ends. Among these were denial-of-service attacks, and just the threat of one allowed the herder to blackmail the potential target. Introducing spyware was not uncommon and allowed the herder to collect the user's passwords, credit card numbers, and banking information all of which would be used to loot his financial accounts. The planted malware might be something so simple as placing ads on the computer without the owner's consent or employing the computer to distribute spam.

The reality was that the herder had at his disposal a vast network of computers he could put to most any use he desired, all without the knowledge of the individual computer owner or operator or both. The NL's vast network had proved highly effective against others but in analyzing the uses to which they were put, Bandeira had determined that such vast networks remained largely untapped as future sources of illicit income.

Marvelous as computers were, though, he was still forced to deal with error-prone people. There was no getting away from it. He'd seen it time and again. Carefully designed systems stumbled because some idiot wrote sloppy code.

Just then, an aide entered quietly, waiting to be acknowledged. "Yes?" Bandeira asked, turning from the window.

"Your son wishes to speak with you. He says it is urgent."

Casas de Férias, Vacation Homes, the operation managed by Pedro, had been slow developing and had been fully operational for only the last year. But careful planning and Ramos's hard work had paid off. It was Bandeira's special pride, and he had high expectations for its long-term success. He'd invested a bundle to make it happen.

The rewards flowed over the wires, bounced around the world, sometimes even into his own bank. This particular cyberoperation was about to turn into a cash cow, one he saw no reason he couldn't keep milking for decades. The only negative he could see was that the millions they were making were small time. Billions of dollars were out there for the taking, it was just up to Ramos to figure out how. Someone, somewhere, was going to manage to steal from the NYSE without detection, why not NL?

"*Padre*," Pedro said. "I'm sorry to report we have a serious problem. It's just come up."

"Tell me."

Pedro laid out what was taking place in New York. He was worked up and Bandeira cautioned him to slow down twice, but he got it all out in the end. "So we've been detected?" Bandeira asked.

"That is what I'm told, though they don't yet seem to know precisely what we are doing."

"Tell me again about the killing."

"This American was instructed to fix the problem he'd caused with sloppy code. His response was to kill the IT manager who stumbled on it."

"That's amazing. He did this on his own?"

"Yes. I'm shocked. I never thought things would go this far. This is a cyberoperation."

Bandeira paused to consider the implications. "Has the body been found?"

"This happened in Chicago. Many killings happen there every week. The manager hasn't been reported missing as yet."

Bandeira suppressed his anger. There was no doubt what he'd do with the American if the man lived in Brazil. To kill without authorization unless in self-defense was absolutely forbidden in his organization. Even now, Bandeira considered dispatching César or one of his special operatives to take care of this. "How crucial is this man in New York?" he asked.

"Vital. He has access to functions we would not have otherwise. As part of his responsibility he is one of those who places code directly into the trading engines."

A weak link Bandeira realized. Could anything have been done about it before now? Shouldn't he have known this man was capable of such independence? And that he was a killer? Ramos should have known.

"Is this the same man who used a stealth program to hide key code?"

"Yes, the same."

"He's reckless and not just with computers. I made it very clear this was to be a cautious, low-key operation. I have planned to run it, or variations of it, for years. That's why I've committed so many resources to it."

"I understand. But . . . I didn't recruit the man. That was Abílio."

"Can he be controlled?"

"I . . . I really don't know. I don't know if any of us could have anticipated something like this. It is all so unexpected."

"All right. I understand. What should we do?" This was not the first time Bandeira had asked his son directly for advice. Whenever possible, he followed it or some version of it. He knew he must build up the young man's confidence and confirm his judgment.

"I'm concerned. I think we're running out of time. We've taken ninety-four million so far, but we were expecting much more. "

"You see no chance this can be kept quiet?"

"I talked with my team here before calling you. As you know the code this man planted is concealed but the fact that it is concealed has been discovered. Abílio doesn't know for certain, but suspects they are tracing our program."

"*Merda.*" Bandeira closed his eyes. Right now, he wanted to have his hands around someone's throat. He'd talk to César. This fool in New York was a dead man. He didn't care how long it took. He drew a deep breath, then released it slowly. "What else do I need to know?"

"That is all I can tell you. Maybe we need to shut down and revisit our options."

Out of the question, Bandeira thought. "I mentioned upping the take on Carnaval next week. You had reservations and so I did not proceed but everything has now changed." He paused to think, and then, as always happened in the face of adversity, a solution came to him. "Pedro, here's what I want you to do. You must trust me in this."

19

This was a rush job, but Marc Campos reminded himself not to be careless because of that. He had enough time to do it right. If he botched this, he'd make the situation worse than it was, and that was the last thing he wanted. Iyers had already made one major coding error, and Campos didn't want to repeat it.

Recruiting him, Campos realized, had been a mistake. He'd thought Iyers a gifted code writer disenchanted with Wall Street, and he was right. The cynicism in his manner and voice when Iyers agreed to join him had been honest indicators of how he truly felt. But obviously there was much more to him than that. The man was *louco*.

In English, he was crazy, psycho. All of them fit. Traveling to Chicago and murdering an IT manager was so out of bounds, so extreme, Campos was still stunned that he'd done it. He'd not even wanted to tell Pedro but knew he had to. So far no one had asked him how such a thing could happen, but he knew he had to have an answer.

Iyers might be nuts—now, there was another word—but when he put his mind to it, he knew how to write code. The remarkable success of Vacation Homes was testament to Iyers's aptitude. He was skilled in the use of the paths through to the deployment server so that their malware blended in, gluing the Brazilian code into the trading engine.

Once Iyers had agreed to work for him, Campos sent to Rio the trading engine source code and software architecture design documents he'd provided. From Rio, Campos received code drops and after reviewing them transferred them to Iyers for insertion.

Campos wondered if something was going on with the man that he should know about, but then dismissed the thought from his mind. Of necessity this project would all be over soon and the damage was done.

Now he'd been instructed to immediately launch Carnaval, in consideration for months. He would set Iyers loose on it; he had to. There was a great deal to do and not much time. Now, more than before, he needed Carnaval to be a great success. His instructions were to make it a hit and for that he required Iyers.

What really angered Campos was the need to bring Vacation Homes, his pet project, to an abrupt close. Yes, the potential payoff from Carnaval was substantial, but he had devoted nearly five years to Vacation Homes, and while it was true that even in the relative short year it was operational, he'd become a rich man, the project had barely scraped its potential. He was convinced they could skim a billion dollars without being detected, and in fact had honestly believed they could take ten times that given enough time, and without Carnaval.

Now this American fool had brought it all to an end. Campos had no doubt what would happen to Iyers once his access and skill were no longer needed. The man had figured out that Campos had a boss. What he didn't imagine was how ruthless the *chefe* was prepared to be. His boss had put great stock in Vacation Homes, and in Carnaval, and would not be happy that a preventable coding error had ended it all before its time. Iyers had been cautioned about how code was to be revised. He'd understood but instead took a shortcut.

And that hadn't been Iyers's only misstep. When they'd first set up accounts to funnel the money out he'd carelessly stolen an identity that too closely resembled his own. He argued that it had been necessary as it was increasingly difficult to set up financial accounts with false identities. Campos had put a stop to his involvement in managing target accounts and now had it all done out of Rio.

As if all that weren't enough, Campos didn't like his hand being forced this way. When Pedro had first suggested Carnaval, it was Campos who'd opposed it. It was too risky he'd argued. It was crafted to exploit an IPO, and they could be very unpredictable. Such a launch might prove too chaotic. Now, on receiving instructions to initiate it immediately, he was convinced more than ever that Carnaval was a step too far. Putting it into place in a rush, aiming for so much, would doom it to failure, he believed. If it unraveled in the worst possible way, he might be caught before he left the country.

Looking up, Campos could see through one of the open office doors around the perimeter to the windows. The nearby taller buildings gleamed in the sunlight, catching rays like a mirror. He'd enjoyed these years in New York City. He regretted he'd not had time to see more of America. Well, he could always come back if he really wanted. But it would be good to be home again.

His mind turned to what he needed to do in the next week. He didn't want to risk staying here much longer. Once Vacation Homes was shut down and especially after Carnaval was finished there'd be hell. Investigators would be swarming everywhere. They could look all they wanted. Marco Campos would vanish. The money would be gone as well.

From his work computer, Campos accessed the Internet using a server and student identity from New York State University, one of a group from the thousands of log-ins that the NL botnets had harvested to which he'd been given access for just these occasions. Students were always hacking each other's identities as pranks or to get back at people for perceived social networking slights. He'd found in the past that a major university was an effective mask for what he was about to do.

He spent a few minutes in research, found two sites that looked right, and was satisfied when he visited the second, which he knew was the most popular. Data Retriever Solutions, or DRS, could have been anywhere from what Campos observed on their Web page. Likely it was physically located somewhere in the United States but its site was set up offshore, and when Campos checked, he saw it was registered to a corporation in Panama—about what he expected.

He'd already established a PayPal account and placed money into it from a throwaway prepaid credit card. Now he entered onto DRS as much information as he had on Jeff Aiken, including his business and residence address. Within seconds, he had his social security number, names of his parents and grandparents, schools he'd attended, his date of birth, which gave him his zodiac sign, even the name of two pets he'd had as a child.

Interesting, Campos thought, wondering where DRS had come by that information. Once he'd written it down, he returned to the first site and did it all again, this time using more of the information he'd just obtained.

Nothing new there. Now he went back to DRS and repeated the process for Red Zoya.

A few minutes later, satisfied, he logged out. He walked down the hallway to the elevators, punched the button for the ground floor, then fingered the disposable cell phone he'd picked up for cash earlier that day. Sometimes, he thought, stepping into the elevator as he smiled at a coworker, technology just made all this too easy.

In the warming sunlight of the fall day Campos sat on a cement bench as he placed the call. Once he had a human voice at the other end, he fumbled the sheets of paper out.

"Yes, I'd like to set up a brokerage account."

20

Jeff had now turned his full attention to reverse engineering the hidden file. He and Frank had discussed this the night before, and though they accomplished what they'd been hired to do and could write their report, neither was satisfied with not knowing what this file did. Successfully reverse engineering it would tell them that. The downside was that not every reverse engineering effort went smoothly or quickly. So while Frank worked on the report and summary of findings, which included their recommendations for enhancing the cybersecurity for NYSE Euronext, Jeff worked on the mysterious software.

Reverse engineering meant taking a bit of software apart starting with the finished product and working backwards. This entailed going from implementation to the development cycle of the code, that is, to the time when it was first written. It was much like disassembling a toaster to see what made it work, except that in the software world, it was a process of examination only and did not involve modifying any of the code. The process wasn't always successful, though with Jeff, it usually was.

Because the file was concealed by a rootkit, he suspected whoever created it didn't want it to be reverse engineered, so he expected obstacles. It might take more time than he could reasonably justify to Stenton, which was one reason he'd hesitated, but he just couldn't resist at least making the effort.

Jeff used a debugger to watch the file execute step by step. Whoever had written the code had, as he suspected, employed anti-debugging mechanisms, common in malware, which were intended to slow down and potentially discourage anyone from reverse engineering the file. Jeff was familiar with nearly all the known ones used, so though it slowed his work, it did not stop him. A software environment was simply too easily manipulated for code obfuscation to serve as a lasting barrier.

After several hours, Frank asked, "How's it going?"

"I don't know yet. I'm pretty sure it's malware and has got something to do with trading. If so, it's extremely sophisticated. But I still can't clearly see what it's meant to do, so I'm not positive."

"You'll figure it out, you always do."

"Not always. I did find a string of numbers inside, but they aren't related to anything, and they don't fit any obvious pattern, at least not to me."

"You sure they aren't money figures?"

"I'm not sure of anything, but my guess is they're identifying something."

"Enjoy."

"You know, the Exchange is lucky they hired us for this pentest. We've uncovered more than they feared was going on. We're giving them more value for this test than they could ever have imagined."

"I'm sure Stenton will be grateful when it comes time to pay up," Frank said with a sly smile.

21

Marc Campos was back in his cubicle and had accessed his computer but that was for show. He had no intention of taking the next step from his own workstation. That's why this part had to be done now, as the place was winding down. A number of workers were taking a break before returning to finish projects due the next day. During the lunch hour and at times such as this, when workers often left their station, planning to return shortly, they didn't always lock their screen. Idle computers required users to log back in after fifteen minutes. He didn't have much time.

Still, this was risky, and he hated its necessity. So far he'd never taken such a significant risk. No, he thought bitterly, Iyers had done that for him.

Standing in his cubicle, Campos scanned the floor. Almost everyone was away from their desk. He rose, then slowly strolled down the hallway until he found an empty cubicle with no one occupying either side. He checked but the screen was locked.

He resumed his stroll and soon popped into another empty cubicle. The computer was unlocked. He sat down.

"Can I help you?"

Campos looked up. "Oh, hi, Rose."

Rose Aquilar was a bit short and growing stout, originally from the Philippines, she already worked at the Exchange when Campos came on board. "Are you lost?"

Campos stood up. "I'm sorry. I was on my way out and realized I'd forgotten to check on something. I saw you were still logged in. I hope you don't mind."

Rose stared at Campos, as if considering her response. "I guess not but I don't like sharing my computer. Your station's not that far away."

Campos stepped into the hallway. "I'm really sorry. My mind was somewhere else. I apologize. It won't happen again."

"All right, then." Rose sat, logged off, stood pointedly, then said, "I'll see you tomorrow."

Campos went into the men's room to give her time to leave the office. He stepped into one of the stalls, his hands shaking violently. That was close. What if she said something? Then he thought a second. Of course she'd say something. She was the office gossip. He should never have risked her station.

After five minutes, he went back out. Rose was nowhere in sight. He walked about the large space, ignoring the stations, confirming that Rose was really gone. He couldn't risk her catching him at someone else's computer but this couldn't wait. Once he'd satisfied himself, he selected a station in the far corner. The user was still logged in but the timer was about to expire.

Campos rapidly downloaded a file from an internal site containing a collection of UTP diagnostic tools, this one with a backdoor he'd embedded that enabled it to execute commands from his own system—in essence, it was a disguised bot. Now he had access to this and other accounts on the network with no trace to his own location or computer. Campos programmed the backdoor so he could monitor the user's connection to the jump server.

That done, Campos left the cubicle and waited for others to leave. He found four computers logged off for the day but located two other connected computers and did the same thing. The sooner someone accessed the secure zone through the jump server, the sooner he'd be finished.

He went back outside, bought a kosher hot dog from a cart, then ate standing up, savoring the moment. When he was finished, he returned to his cubicle and his own computer. One of the users he hacked was in the process of accessing the jump server as Campos had anticipated. Break time was over, time to get back to work. He piggybacked into the secure zone, leaving no trace of himself.

Now Campos meticulously searched for signs of Red Zoya and the specialized tools Jeff and Frank used in their work. He smiled slightly as he did. Satisfied at what he saw he planted in a version of Iyers's trade manipulation malware very similar to the one used for Vacation Homes. Once that was in place, he dropped in the program he'd configured to blatantly manipulate trades, making no attempt at concealment. He set it up so the money skimmed from trades was moved into the brokerage account that he'd established earlier for Jeff. As an automated security measure the malware was programmed to delete part of itself and in so doing it extracted one of Jeff's free cybersecurity tools, exposing it to view. This behavior Campos knew would trigger the antivirus program when it performed its next routine scan.

From this moment on, Vacation Homes would look as if it was Jeff Aiken's pride and joy. Gotta love computers, Campos thought as he backed out of the secure zone. Now it was up to the Exchange's IT sleuths and the software they had implanted, which hunted for just this sort of thing.

With this done Campos went in search of Iyers to discuss Carnaval. Everything had to move like clockwork from this point on.

DAY FOUR
THURSDAY, SEPTEMBER 13

HIGH-FREQUENCY TRADING UNDER SCRUTINY

HFTs Alleged to Harm Markets

By Frederick Z. Isaacs
September 13

Computers have reduced costs, increased participation, and improved the efficiency of stock markets the world over, according to the annual report of the Institute for Market Awareness. In its just-released report, institute president Arlene Bliss wrote that computers have linked exchanges, streamlined trading, and accelerated the flow of information, all of which has served the best interests of investors. But the report also cautioned that for all the good computing has brought to securities trading, it is now being used in ways not previously anticipated. The primary culprit is high-frequency trading while the driving principle is unparalleled greed.

HFT, as it is known, exploits the ability of supercomputers to execute trading opportunities in nanoseconds. Their highly sophisticated algorithms seek out price differences, then buy and sell at unbelievable speeds. The secret algorithms are referred to as Black Boxes.

Now that they dominate most major trades high-frequency trading companies are seeking new ways to leverage their advantage. The NYSE for one makes this easy by allowing new algos to be tested on their system without notifying them. More than once, such tests have caused serious disruptions in regular trading yet they are still permitted. In addition the NYSE allows HFTs to buy proximity location beside its super engines, giving them an advantage that others cannot exploit.

Competition with other exchanges is cited as the reason for NYSE behavior. "Administrators believe that if they do not allow proximity location or the testing of sophisticated algos other exchanges will and the NYSE will lose its advantageous place in world trading," the report says.

Critics point out that such measures create tension between the need for security within the trading platform and the desire by the NYSE to serve the demands of its major, and favored, players. "While playing favorites raises the issue of fundamental fairness," Clara Derns of the Investors Action League says, "its willingness to accept freewheeling algos and to grant favored access is courting disaster. The day is coming when the system will suffer a cataclysmic collapse because of high-frequency trading. It is inevitable given the current practices of the NYSE."

According to the report, "NYSE is confident that high-frequency trading can be effectively managed. There is no reason for undue alarm." The report concludes that such optimism is unwarranted.

Everyone in the industry knows that new regulatory controls are coming. While it is unlikely they will end the abuses of HFTs they will certainly make their current practices more difficult. In retrospect, these may well be seen as the halcyon days. The consequence is that greed is sure to drive these mysterious traders to even more extreme actions, which could create worldwide economic instability.

Bliss declined comment beyond what is contained in the institute's annual report, adding only that she has grave personal concerns about the future for traditional market investors.

Internet News Service, Inc.

22

Pedro Bandeira entered the company office and was taken at once by the sense of urgency. His three employees were in their cubicles, each working intensely on their computers. He nodded in satisfaction as he passed through to his corner office opposite the door. Preparations to launch Carnaval were in full swing now. What had been a new dimension of the ongoing effort, one intended to be brought out for each major IPO, had in a single conversation become the primary effort. And his father's orders were explicit: Get as much as possible, then vanish and cover their tracks. He wanted no less than a $10 billion payday in under one week.

Ten billion dollars.

Pedro could scarcely conceive of such a sum. To take so much, in so short a time, to move it away safely, all was a challenge and no one involved was convinced it was possible. But he was determined to do this right, to make it the crowning success his father wanted.

Located a few blocks from the famous Maracanã football stadium, the office for the generically named Grupo Técnico was housed in a former mansion. Built at the turn of the last century it was a simplified form of the classic Portuguese Baroque style. When the wealthy abandoned this quarter of Rio, the building had been converted into apartments for a decade, then reconverted into office space. One of the cartel's legitimate companies had acquired the building, then remodeled it for Grupo Técnico, which used only the second floor.

A reception desk sat before the two enormous French doors of the main entrance. It was here the interior guard normally sat with his surveillance monitor. Behind his chair was a waiting area with two burnt orange–colored overstuffed chairs and a matching couch. To the left were doors to break and storage rooms. The right side consisted of the wall, still displaying the original murals of romantic country scenes, the colors now faded to irregular pastels, with long windows overlooking the exterior, where an English-style garden had once been. To the rear of the salon and to the left of the couch was a rear door. On the other side was the staircase, which turned once at an angle to the right, leading up to a landing. Around the second floor was a narrow mezzanine that led to the former bedrooms and living quarters. The Grupo Técnico offices were at the immediate top of the landing, where they had a clear view to the large room below.

The building was set just back from the center of a large square parcel of green. For security concerns, the overgrown trees had been removed along with the shrubbery. Nothing remained of the former luscious garden but a flat expanse of grass broken only by a single asphalt driveway ending in a circle at the front doors. In the rear, to one side, was a helicopter landing pad, occasionally used by Victor Bandeira. On the opposite side of the lot was a long low structure, once a horse stable, that now stored gardening tools.

The grounds were surrounded in typical Brazilian practice by a high block wall topped first with glass and metal spikes, then with four feet of electrified wire. The building itself was visible from the street only through the oversized ornate automatic metal doors for cars. Beside them was a door for pedestrians while just inside was a sentry box, concealed within the compound.

Security cameras, with night-vision capability, covered both the exterior and interior. The monitors were manned on the first floor twenty-four hours a day. In addition to the sentry there was always at least one guard on foot on the grounds of the mansion and within able to respond on a moment's notice. Three in all, four if you counted the entrance sentry present during the usual workday. For all this, the security was discreet and nothing to the outward eye brought attention to the company.

Pedro lived within walking distance of his office near the Quinta da Boa Vista, the park where the historic Imperial Palace was located. This wasn't the very best part of Rio but it was nice enough for his taste. He disdained the ostentatious lifestyle of some of those he'd grown up with and often found his father's pretension an embarrassment.

Pedro had successfully managed to keep surveillance cameras out of the work area and the rear patio, where he and his staff took breaks. César came by from time to time for a security inspection. There was nothing Pedro could say to prevent that.

For all this the security was not really all that much greater than for many businesses in Rio, where theft was institutionalized. Uniformed armed guards were a common sight and Pedro could have named any number of businesses with significantly greater security.

Lunch with his father had brought no new information, though perhaps a bit of insight. Pedro's mother had already told him the truth about his father years before. Even then, it had come as no surprise. He'd known since childhood that his father was senior in the Nosso Lugar cartel in São Paulo, later *chefe*. His school friends told him, and at first, it had been like being told there was no Papai Noel. He respected and adored his father. To learn he was a criminal had been the cause of more than one school fight.

In the end, he'd decided that it was of no concern to him. He led his own life, let his father live his. Then, like a thunderbolt, had come the divorce. There'd been some divorces among the parents of other students but it was rare, and frowned upon. The children of such families were taunted.

Angry, and over his father's objections, Pedro had dropped out of school. The more the man insisted he return, the more determined Pedro was to stay out. More than once, he'd dared his father to hit him as Brazilian fathers had a right to do but the man resisted, though clearly he'd been tempted. The worst times were at the family house, which his father had kept in the divorce on a day when one of his mistresses was there. These were women younger than Pedro, women who'd given him the "look" as his friends called it, telling him they were available if he was interested.

It was disgusting. How could his father abandon his wife for such women? To keep them on the side, out of sight, that was tolerable, but this . . .

Pedro had been more driven than ever, spending his nights in upscale nightclubs, drinking and smoking too much, indulging in soft drugs, engaging in careless sex, angry, headed for trouble. Finally, his mother had confronted him, persuaded him to return to school, then later, to work for his father.

"You are his only son," she said. "You must."

"The only son you know about," he'd answered, his eyes slipping away from hers as he spoke, regretting his words at once.

Esmeralda hadn't missed a beat. "You are his only son by his wife and that is what matters."

Pedro had consented as much out of curiosity as obedience. Anyway, he was sick of the life he was leading. What, he wondered, did his father really do? Yes, he was a criminal but in Brazil that could mean many things. Were the stories of drugs, prostitutes, and extortion true? His classmates had no doubt. His father said he was a banker. At least that's where his office was. Pedro had met the president of the republic there. He'd met other important figures as well. Did such men associate with *chefes*? And why his interest in computers? Could his claim that he wanted Pedro to run a legitimate company be true?

The only real surprise at the lunch was learning how his grandparents had died and that he'd once had an aunt. He'd been shocked to hear his father speak in that gutter dialogue of the favelas, impressed with the way he shed it so easily and returned to his usual speech. Leaving the house afterwards, he'd wondered which was real. In which language did his father think?

Renata Oliveira entered his office. "We're already having trouble with Carnaval. I'm really concerned." In her early thirties, Renata was a single mother. She was nothing but business in the office. With average looks she was in no danger of turning heads and neither of the two male employees had ever shown an interest in her, for which Pedro was grateful. She was steady and very hardworking.

"What kind of trouble?"

She took a chair and scanned her notes. "The trade matching engine code in New Jersey has been updated, and we're having to take time away from Carnaval to adapt our code."

"We've done that before."

"Yes, but never with so much more that has to be done and very little time. The major problem with Carnaval is we have to wait for the next update to get our revised code in. There's only one scheduled between now and next Wednesday. There might be more given the problems they seem to be having, but we have only one definite shot and have to hit that mark."

"Can we?"

Renata looked uncertain, then said, "I think so. We're also busy creating dozens of holding accounts with multiple layers of misdirection through which to funnel the money. But it's a lot, much more than Carnaval was intended for originally, and we almost can't have too many of these. I'd feel better if we had hundreds. But I worry about mistakes with that and the coding. Everyone's tired and going to get even more tired before we are finished. Most of the team has been up since you told us the new priority."

"The confusion and activity of the IPO will help to hide us."

"Of course, but we can't depend on that alone."

No news there, Pedro thought. "So how's it coming?"

Renata looked nervous. "Slowly I'm afraid. But we're working flat out."

"Whatever you come up with will have to do." His mouth turned dry. "What else?"

"With the target number you've given us we can only get half from the IPO without having the Exchange shutting it down. We're running analysis to identify the high-volume, highly volatile stocks we need for the non-IPO companies we can exploit through Vacation Homes. Again, we need a lot of them so when we pull out money, it will appear anomalous. We require very specific stocks to make this part work. I could use ten more people."

"That's not possible. But I'm back and will work with you. We'll make it. You'll see."

Renata nodded, looking doubtful, then returned to her desk and went to work.

It was times like this when Pedro really felt in charge of the company. At first, Abílio Ramos had been the actual boss. No one had said it, but Pedro understood. He'd set up his father's gambling operation, even spending time in Costa Rica until he had run afoul of authorities. After that the operation had become fully computerized with operations spread worldwide, serving more as the middlemen for the major online gaming operations. Ramos had done a good job from what Pedro knew, and at first, he'd been a bit in awe of the man.

Even after Ramos had left Brazil, the two had talked nearly every day and still did before Pedro's team did anything significant. Pedro's father required it. "We must be on the same page," he said.

Pedro could see the truth of that as what they did was complicated; not just the doing, but the concealing. Yet it still irritated him that he had to check in with Ramos. Now that they were in the final phases of the biggest operation yet he and Ramos communicated every few hours.

Pedro leaned back in his chair. Ten billion dollars. Was such a sum even possible? He'd expected to work at Casas de Férias, Vacation Homes, for at least another four or five years and anticipated taking perhaps a billion dollars over that time. That had seemed like a lot to him.

Now to learn he must increase the take ten times and set it up within one week, execute it on a single day, within the window of a few short hours, was almost overwhelming. But he'd been fascinated at the prospect. The systems were in place. They had plenty of experience moving the money and hiding their tracks. And the code his people had devised was elegant, beautiful to watch operate.

What would taking such an amount do to the world financial markets? Casas de Férias had been created on the assumption that money would be removed from many unrelated transactions, spread over time and distance. Any one company would feel the pinch but the high volume of trading activity, the usual fluctuations in price, would serve to mask what was going on. If anyone suspected what had happened, they'd be a lone voice complaining about it. The Exchange wasn't going to admit that an operation like Casas de Férias was possible, that their Holy Grail, their servers, had been hacked. Not even if they found the code, not even then would they acknowledge it. No, the beauty of what NL did was that their primary target would ultimately work just as hard to hide what they'd done as they did. It was like burglarizing a mansion knowing the owner would never call the police.

But Pedro's gut, his common sense and his experience, told him that $10 billion in a single day was too much, too risky. Even Ramos, so devoted to his father, had expressed reservations. Would the Exchange conceal a loss of such magnitude? Could it even manage to?

But this wasn't his concern, Pedro reminded himself. He had his instructions. What rankled was the necessity. He still had no idea what had gone wrong. Ramos had said nothing to him nor had his father but something had. Five years they'd been at this, four of them to set it up, to begin earning, and now this.

It was someone, Pedro thought. Not code error but human error. It had to be. That was nearly always the way. The fewer people involved with an operation like this, the less likely there'd be a mistake. But they'd never have pulled it off without inside help and that was always the weakest link.

For all the interest Pedro had in the outcome, for all the money he and his team would make, for the satisfaction he'd feel at pleasing his father and mother, he had already decided to walk away. He'd thought he'd be at this another few years. Now he realized he could leave within a few weeks. The reality had come to him the night before, as he'd gone to bed and his excited thoughts at the pending prospect had kept him awake until almost dawn.

The fact was that he didn't want to be a criminal. He'd watched his father closely since coming to work for him. True, he lived an opulent life and exercised great power, probably more than he realized Pedro knew, but how could he sleep at night? How could he live constantly looking over his shoulder, with César and his men always there? That wasn't the life Pedro wanted for himself.

The pressure of Carnaval and the expanded Casas de Férias was bringing his fears and suppressed aspirations to the surface in ways he'd never experienced before. He had friends who had no idea who he was. That was one reason why he'd insisted in locating the company in Rio, away from his father's interests. He'd also insisted the company be legitimate from all appearances, that it conduct itself exactly as a legal operation did. He liked being accepted for who he really was, not treated with respect by those wanting favor with his father. He'd had too much of that in his life.

And he needed to leave soon he'd decided, which meant Carnaval was an opportunity. The longer he stayed, the more deeply he'd be pulled into his father's world.

Pedro turned to his screen as he heard the familiar Skype sound. Ramos wanted to talk. Pedro sighed, pressing back in his mind the one nagging thought he'd had since lunch the previous day.

Would his father let him go?

23

ENFORCEMENT DIVISION
SECURITIES AND EXCHANGE COMMISSION
NEW YORK REGIONAL OFFICE
200 VESSEY STREET
NEW YORK CITY
4:01 P.M.

Robert Alshon, senior SEC investigator, picked up the telephone. "Susan? Could you come by my office at once? Thank you."

Alshon was busy with the printed sheets in front of him when Susan Flores knocked lightly at his office door. She came in and sat down in an armed chair in front of his desk. She was not yet thirty years old, single, of average size with long jet black hair. She was part of Alshon's team but was more than a little intimidated by him. His expectations were always difficult. She raised an eyebrow.

"We've got a hot one from the SSG at the Exchange." SSG was the Server Systems Group of the Infrastructure Management Department of the New York Stock Exchange. They were the digital cops responsible for detecting irregularities within the code, but especially potential criminal conduct. Alshon met her eyes with that same intensity he always showed at the beginning of a chase. Forty years old, formerly with the Federal Bureau of Investigation before joining the SEC, he handled "big ticket" cases of insider or fraudulent trading. He was broad shouldered, with short clipped graying hair and a trim black mustache. He was known as a bulldog for his relentless investigations and attention to detail. Arrogant and on occasion nasty he was the best and Flores considered herself lucky to be part of his investigation team.

"They're still at it, so we've got a chance to catch them red-handed," Alshon continued with obvious pleasure.

"How big?" she asked. When it came to securities, she'd once told a girlfriend, size was everything.

"I can't say at this point. That's one reason I want you on this. The scope is extensive. A rough guess would be in the neighborhood of eight to twelve million dollars, though if it was twice that, I wouldn't be surprised."

"How long?"

"They don't know; likely only a few weeks. It's a pretty clever operation but then they're exploiting a position of trust. That always makes access easy."

"What do we know?"

Alshon leaned back in his chair. "Some weeks ago, Stenton's team spotted a random bot on their system. It was one of those auto-spreading robot things that never should have got by their defenses. They were due for a penetration test so decided to bring in an outside team, someone new for a fresh approach. They hired some genius out of D.C."

"I read about the bot on the way in this morning. Who'd they hire?"

Alshon looked back at the report. "Jeffrey Aiken, Red Zoya. Know it?"

"Not the company but the name sounds familiar. It will come to me."

"I'm talking to Gene when we finish and will have him get me all the info on this Aiken guy and his company." Gene Livingston was the team's primary researcher. "Anyway, it seems they've had some success and a few days ago penetrated the New Jersey engines."

"Wow. They tell me that isn't possible. How long did it take?"

Alshon grimaced. "Something like two weeks."

"That's impressive."

"Maybe not. They may have been working on this for a while."

"If that's true, it's quite a coincidence them getting hired for the penetration test."

"Good point." Alshon leaned forward and wrote a quick note to himself. "Maybe there's more here than meets the eye. Bill Stenton hired them. I'll have Gene look for a connection."

"Bill's clean I'm sure."

Alshon smirked. "Trust me. You never know. Anyway, IT says they've been inside a few days but—now, get this—they've not reported the penetration. And they've been doing some very funny things in there too."

"You know the timing is interesting."

"How's that?"

"There've been reports for months now from brokers about unexpected losses."

"They're always complaining, looking for someone to blame."

"I know, but I understand Bill has received a series of complaints about trades coming in well under projection. He's been looking into it. Maybe that was the real reason for the test."

"How much are brokers reporting?"

Flores shook her head. "I don't have figures but I understand it's in the tens of millions, more than a million per incident in some cases."

Alshon made another note. "I'll have Stenton prepare a report for me of these incidents once we clear him and tell him what we're up to."

"What do you want me to do?"

"I'm forwarding the IT report to you. You've got access. I want you to go in there and take a look at what they're up to, confirm suspicions. I don't like trusting an outside party. Be sure they don't see you in there. In the meantime I'll turn Gene loose. I'm going to move fast on this one. My gut tells me we don't have a lot of time. It'll be good to catch them in the act. We'll talk next morning. You've got a long night ahead of you."

"All right. When is this penetration test supposed to wrap up?"

"They don't know. It should already be finished, but like I say, they're still in there, doing God knows what."

"All right." Flores stood up and moved toward the door, then stopped and looked back. "You know, sir, there could be a good reason why they haven't reported penetration yet. That by itself isn't suspicious."

"Read the report," Alshon said with an edge. "There's two of them on the team. They're a nasty piece of work. They're both ex-Company men. I've had experience with this kind before." He glanced at his wristwatch. "Stay on this and keep me updated. I'm catching the shuttle to D.C."

24

I'm having a beer. Want one?" Frank asked as he went to the minibar in his room.

Jeff shook his head as he sat. Frank passed him a bottle of water. "Let me tell you where I am. I still don't know what those numbers in the hidden file mean, but I'm filling in the holes around them. I've been focusing on what the code does. It looks like it interacts with another component on the trading servers. It seems to search for particular conditions within defined trades, then takes part."

"And it's malware."

"Absolutely."

"So whatever it's doing is bad. Sounds like it's taking money. What else would malware be doing within the Exchange's trading engines?"

"Almost certainly, one way or another. I suspect that it's found a way to get into legitimate trades and take a piece of the action. I can't be sure, but I think that's it. Everything fits."

"If it did that, the Exchange's security would catch it."

"I think it's more sophisticated than that."

"Those numbers might be accounts. Maybe those it accesses or where it sends the trades."

"That's what I'm thinking, but they could be anything. I'm hoping to puzzle it out tomorrow. I know we need to close this engagement out but I really want to understand what is taking place."

"The report's about finished, except for what you're doing. Do you have a meeting set?"

"I called to schedule it," Jeff said.

"When?"

"His secretary's supposed to get back to me."

"Is Stenton out of town?"

"I don't know."

"You'd think he'd want to hear what we have to say. Did you read the *Times* today?" Frank gestured at the copy he'd picked up earlier. Jeff shook his head. "The bot that got us this gig is in the news, in the financial section. According to the article, a former Exchange employee revealed all the details, and there's a fracas since the New York Stock Exchange security is supposed to be the best in the world."

"The bot was harmless."

"Not according to the article. The ex-employee is claiming all kinds of damage has been done and the Exchange, in particular Stenton, is covering it up. The article suggests that the extent of the malware is vast."

"Wow."

"And the stock market tanked today, down something like ten percent, a record of some kind."

"Think about what would happen if they knew what we'd found."

"Jeff, imagine what would happen if they knew what we've managed to do in such a short time." Frank paused, then continued, "Stenton told you this pentest was urgent, and it turns out he was more than right. Just the two of us pulled penetration off, Jeff. Think about it. We might be geniuses, at least that's what I tell my wife, but there are plenty of bright geeks out there. If we can do it, so can they. How many others have got in there? For all we know the Exchange computers are leaking like a sieve. Stenton needs to hear that, and see how we did it. Just from what we've found they've got a lot of holes to close and procedures to tighten. That's especially true with the heat turned up."

"Yeah." Jeff shrugged. "I understand but if he's in no hurry to get our report, that's fine with me. In my opinion, this malware is more important than the fact we managed the penetration, especially now. I think we need to know what's going on before we report. Another day should give us some answers. We've worked pretty fast so we've got the time."

They sat in silence for a bit; then Frank said, "What? You've got that look."

"Nothing really."

"Come on."

"I'm probably just reading something from nothing. But Stenton's secretary sounded . . . I don't know . . . uneasy. I can't put my finger on it. I was probably just tired."

Frank grunted. "Now that you mention it I've caught a few looks in the hallway."

"What do you mean?"

"Nothing that registered at the time, just looks. Is something going on we don't know about?"

Jeff shrugged. "If we don't know about it, how would I know?" He grinned. "You sound paranoid."

Frank sighed. "I just want to get home. I miss everybody."

"Well, I'm going for a run. We'll save the world financial system tomorrow, then get back to our lives."

25

Jeff finished his first lap of the Lower Track. He hadn't run enough since coming to New York. Only now were the kinks easing out of his body. As he reached his start point, he picked up his pace, settling into the mile-eating stride he ran back home.

This project was turning out to be much larger than he'd anticipated. He'd been flattered when Stenton first contacted him. Though Red Zoya had done work for other well-known institutions, most of what it did was behind the scenes, often not even known in the cybersecurity community. An engagement such as this was very high profile. Their successful penetration of the trading platform of the New York Stock Exchange would get out, he had no doubt. Even though there was a standard confidentiality clause in the contract, one he would keep, a number of employees at the Exchange would know what they'd done, they'd chat about it through social media and post their thoughts online. Word would spread and the result would be even more high-profile projects, and though money wasn't primarily what this was all about, it was an important component. If what he thought was about to happen took place, he'd need to expand.

Which returned his thoughts to Daryl. If he was going to build Red Zoya, there was no one else he wanted to build it with. Even Frank for all his expertise and abilities was at heart a family man and at this point in his career could not be expected to give the time to the company such an expansion would demand. As Jeff thought about how to do this his mind returned again and again to Daryl. Her ability, her contacts, how they worked together were simply perfect.

The other side of all this was the idea that maybe he'd been wrong about them. Everyone who knew the two of them told him he'd made a mistake. Sometimes outsiders see things more clearly than those involved do. Wasn't that the nature of a pentest after all? You take for granted what you know. It's someone on the outside who can see the strengths, and weaknesses, clearly. Maybe the fact that he had had no interest in anyone else during the past year was telling him something.

As Jeff finished his second lap, he picked up the pace again. Would Daryl even want to come back? Was there any point in considering it? For a second he thought about presenting it to her as a strictly business proposition. Red Zoya needed her, they worked well together, with their combined experience and contacts the company would thrive.

He almost laughed out loud at the thought. No, if they got together again, it wouldn't be only as business partners. At the least there was too much history. And there was no denying the strong mutual physical attraction. A purely professional relationship, at least for him, would be out of the question.

So what to do? What if she was seeing someone? Or living with someone? His heart sank at the thought.

The fact that she hadn't contacted him, even professionally, in the last year had come as a surprise. When he'd last talked to her that night at the town house, he'd never meant they'd have nothing to do with each other in the future. In fact, he'd been sincere when he said they'd remain friends. After all, they'd been colleagues and friends before they were partners and lovers, why couldn't they return to that? It had seemed reasonable to him.

Then there'd been this long, unsettling silence. Jeff realized that for months he'd been looking for an e-mail or text message from her. Maybe, he thought, she'd been doing the same thing.

Richard Iyers stood concealed in the heavy brush as he watched the runners on the pathway. Jeff had been bunched with three others his first lap, but he pulled away during the second, and when Iyers last saw him, he'd been alone, no one in front of him or behind.

The day he'd made his decision, Iyers considered how to go about this. A mugging on the streets had immediately come to mind. They were common enough in Manhattan but the more he'd considered the risks associated with it, the less appeal it held.

The answer had come to him when he recalled Jeff casually mentioning his run in Central Park on Monday. Iyers recalled that he'd said he was going to run. He'd even mentioned his preference for the Bridle Path because of its forgiving surface.

Iyers had come to the park and scouted the Bridle Path carefully, initially selecting three locations he thought suitable. This was ideal, not far from where it ran beside East Drive. He'd come upon a stout branch, stripped it of its lesser limbs, then secreted it at the location, smiling as he did, recalling how things had gone in Chicago earlier that week.

After that, Iyers had done his best to follow Jeff. He'd waited outside the man's hotel in the morning, followed him after work in the evening. Iyers was reconsidering his decision not to mug him when he'd seen him emerge from his hotel dressed for a run. Iyers had taken a taxi to the park, then gone to his position.

Watching Jeff approach from the distance, he felt a tingle at the thought of what he was about to do. There'd been no word on the other guy. Every day he'd gone to the Chicago news sites, but so far there was no report of a body found at Waterfall Glen. That had come as no surprise. He'd sunk the body deep and weighted it well.

Iyers moved his gloved hand along the length of the branch he held beside him. He'd considered a gun but just as quickly dismissed the idea. He didn't own one and getting a gun, legally or illegally, was too risky. It meant witnesses. He'd not used a firearm in Illinois, because he'd not wanted to attract any notice, and it was no different here.

He'd thought about a knife, a big one, but he'd never stabbed anyone before and had no idea how to go about it. Could he do it silently? He didn't think so. He also knew it would be bloody as well, leaving telltale marks on him. A knife was out of the question.

No, this was best. A victim with a shattered skull in Central Park was not an anomaly. Jaded New Yorkers wouldn't give it a second thought, and the park police would focus on the vagrants who spent their days in the park.

Iyers finished his cigarette, extinguished it on the ground, then slipped it into his pocket before pulling the ski mask over his face.

———

Jeff decided his fourth lap would be his last. He needed to focus on work. If he couldn't see Stenton the next day, and he wasn't in on Saturday, he and Frank would wrap up their work over the weekend and finalize their report for Monday. He hoped that was the way it worked out. He really wanted to solve the mystery of the rogue code himself and make it the crowning discovery of their report.

He wondered what the reaction would be. He and Frank had done more than successfully penetrate the trading platform; they'd discovered what was almost certainly an ongoing criminal operation set up to loot money. That conclusion was a bit of a stretch based on the evidence they had today, but Jeff had no doubt that by Monday, he'd have it nailed down. If the stock market fell over a harmless bot, what would the consequence be if what they'd discovered ever got out?

With an open stretch in front of him and recalling how stable the footing was along this part of the path, Jeff accelerated into his final kick. His side began to ache, and his lungs started to burn, reminding him again that he wasn't running often enough.

Just as he passed a thick cluster of shrubbery his peripheral vision caught sight of a tall figure with a covered face stepping toward him, brandishing something long in his hand. Jeff partially turned, then instinctively veered away and broke into a sprint. There was a sharp brush along his body. He reached East Drive and spotted a police car parked on the other side of the street. Jeff leaped over the low wooden railing to run toward it.

East Drive was closed to traffic most of the time but was open for four hours on weekdays, ending in just a few minutes. The speed limit was twenty-five miles per hour, though speeding cars were not uncommon. The road was clear as Jeff ran in front of a slow-moving vehicle, but he didn't see the speedster racing up beside it. He felt the impact, dull, vague but powerful. His footing slipped away as he lost control of his physical self; then his vision was a series of still frames flashing one after another as he flew through the air.

DAY FIVE
FRIDAY, SEPTEMBER 14

NYSE AFTER THE KNIGHT CAPITAL DISASTER

By Alice Payton

September 14, 10:10 A.M. EST, Updated 11:50 P.M. EST

Toronto—IPO disasters are becoming too common, according to Ryan Brodie, publisher of the popular cybertrading newsletter, *Lightning*. "There is no reason for so many IPOs turning out badly. No reason except greed." Focusing on the 2012 Knight Capital disaster Brodie suggested that the source of the problem is the cozy relationship between high-frequency traders and the NYSE.

The introduction of computers into trading once promised an end to traditional abuses. Instead, the Exchange suffers from continuing issues surrounding the true nature of trades as well as the use of computers and software in accomplishing them. The persistent problems are not all that different from those that traditionally plagued securities trading. For all its sophistication and technical marvel the NYSE remains primarily an exchange of stock for money, the price responding to the universal law of supply and demand. Computers have modified the system but only in kind, not in purpose. But, according to Brodie, too many of the current problems are being caused by computers.

Taking Knight Capital Group as an example, Brodie pointed out that the global financial services firm went nearly bankrupt within the space of a few short hours when its own new code ran amok on the Exchange. The company served as a dealer in securities where investors could trade, at a guaranteed price. Responding to Exchange changes in several kinds of transactions Knight Capital created a special code it then unleashed in secret for a weeklong test trial. What happened next was unintended as legacy software was inadvertently reactivated. The new program proceeded to adversely affect the routing of shares of more than 140 stocks. The consequence was that the company sent repeated erroneous orders. Stock prices swung wildly in a very short time period. What was occurring was that the bad code bought high and sold low, a reversal of what was intended. And it did so in blasts of high-frequency trading lasting less than a few seconds. Worse, it just kept doing it, compressing what was meant to be a long-term test into frenzied action taking place within a few short hours. Knight Capital immediately lost $440 million while its own stock plummeted, losing three quarters of its value in just 48 hours.

This chaos occurred just two years after the infamous Flash Crash and followed a number of high-profile technical glitches. One of these had been the botched Facebook IPO while another had been the failed public offering of BATS.

"It raises serious concerns as to the future of trading," Brodie said. "I really question whether or not any private investor should even be in the stock market at this volatile time." Alternative markets are being regularly created and Brodie said investors should give serious thought to moving their money into these. "Provided they continue excluding high-frequency traders."

Global Computer News Service

26

Richard Iyers went into the restroom and splashed cold water on his face repeatedly. He'd awakened later than usual that morning. He felt awful and wondered if he'd caught a bug. He'd considered not coming into work but reasoned there were potential circumstances where that would seem suspicious. Plus he wanted to know the outcome of his attack. Before leaving his apartment he'd checked the news. All he found was the bare mention that a Central Park jogger had been struck by a speeding car when he strayed onto East Drive. There were no details as to the extent of the injuries.

Iyers wondered if Aiken had been killed. Probably not. The news said nothing about the jogger having died.

On his office floor, something seemed odd this morning. Coworkers were talking in hushed voices in the common areas as he'd entered. There was a slight buzz in the air. He considered going to the break room but decided it was better to show no interest. He'd know soon enough what was up; no need to draw attention to himself by asking.

Iyers had found he was unable to concentrate on work and went to the restroom. He dried his face with paper towels, ran his hands through his hair, then stepped out into the hallway. On the way back to his office, he wandered down the hallway to the office Jeff and Frank used. It was empty. He wondered again if asking about them would be risky, and decided it would be.

Looking back on the previous night, he was filled with recrimination.

He'd exposed himself too much. And he hadn't killed the man. He wondered if anyone had noticed the reason the runner bolted into traffic. If so, there'd be a description, though that didn't especially concern him. It would match many men, considering how he'd dressed.

After he left the park, he'd ditched the mask first, then the coat. He'd disciplined himself to walk carefully and blend in. At the first well-lit location, he'd stopped and casually examined his clothing. There were leaves and small twigs attached to his pants. He'd carefully brushed them away.

When he killed the Italian, he'd experienced nothing but elation. In fact, he'd left the park in such an exalted mood, he knew he'd been careless. On the trip back he'd relived the experience in his thoughts, again and again, relishing every memory. He'd not come to earth until he'd reached Manhattan.

But last night as he fled, he'd felt nothing but fear. The fear was still there, masked only in part by the widespread discomfort he experienced.

At his desk Iyers accessed the logs for the jump servers, the deployment servers, and those of his own system as he did routinely. It occurred to him when he'd first agreed to help Campos that if they could do this, so could someone else. More important, if anyone was investigating what was going on in the system, Iyers would find their tracks here, so several times a day, like someone looking behind him to see if he was being followed, he checked the servers. Nothing.

He wondered what Campos would say when he found out about Aiken. The news report hadn't given a name or mentioned an attack in the park. Would Campos assume it was a coincidence, this happening so soon after they'd discussed it? Not likely but Iyers doubted the man would react at all. He was positive there was an unspoken agreement, an acknowledgment that this act was necessary. No, Campos understood it was necessary, now with Carnaval and Vacation Homes moving into high gear.

Iyers's primary concern was the money. He'd already earned a couple of million but had, as originally agreed, only received small payments. Campos held the balance. It wasn't due yet but now everything was different. With Carnaval he would earn, what? Millions more, for certain. Many millions.

How long would he have to stay on the job after that? If he just vanished, he'd be a suspect as the investigation would definitely come to his department. Anyway, he would want to be here, keep an eye on it, ready to bolt if it turned toward him. Sit, watch, and wait, that was the ticket.

The primary problem was the money. Campos had been long on talk and promises, slow to give him his due, especially now that Carnaval had been vastly expanded. The earnings were going to skyrocket. Iyers didn't like getting so little to date. In fact, he didn't like Campos all that much. He was a weak man, too risk averse. He wasn't willing to do what had to be done. Weak men were dangerous when someone turned up the heat. But Campos was his means of payment; there was nothing to be done about that.

Iyers wondered if he shouldn't already have another identity. In movies, that was easily done while in reality a false identity that passed muster was not so simple. It would be better if he could keep his own, but he wondered now if that would be possible. He'd heard you could get one in Canada without too much trouble. He was from Upstate New York and could talk like a Canadian if need be. Maybe he'd just go there if things got hot, work on another identity then.

But it always came back to the money. He didn't have it except in his dreams. And did Campos ever intend to pay him? He'd often wondered about that. Once he'd determined that his colleague was really just the front man for a much bigger operation he'd been concerned that someone higher up in the food chain might decide it was easier just to take him out. After all, Iyers knew everything. They'd worry he'd flip if caught, and they'd save a bundle by not having to pay him.

No, he'd have to insist he be paid as soon as Carnaval was finished. Insist. He had his personal bank accounts set up, and his tracks were well covered. He was confident about that. He'd seen to it right away in anticipation of unfulfilled paydays.

There was always blackmail, of course, but what could he do if Campos just vanished? Iyers gritted his teeth in exasperation. He had to get more money while he was still needed. He couldn't afford to wait until the end. There had to be a way.

27

Robert Alshon stepped from the black SUV and stood on the sidewalk, slipping on a pair of sunglasses against the surprisingly bright fall afternoon sun. He felt more than a little self-conscious wearing a blue Windbreaker over his white shirt and dark tie. Printed across the back in white letters were the words: SEC ENFORCEMENT DIVISION. In a second line was the word: POLICE.

There'd been a time when that wasn't necessary. He recalled his early raids when he and his then boss had arrived at an office in business suits, displaying the subpoena to the receptionist, meeting briefly with the in-house counsel where they served it, followed by a quick face-to-face with the target, who was promptly told by his attorney to say nothing and cooperate. Alshon's team had then methodically gathered records, typically with the assistance of the company employees. It had all been very polite, cordial, and respectful. Such investigations had taken years and rarely resulted in a jail sentence. That was the way of it, frustrating as he often found the outcome.

But over time, federal law enforcement had changed, and he was glad of it. The old ways had been soft and tolerant. With the Patriot Act and the acts of domestic terrorism no one took chances these days. They couldn't afford to even when serving a subpoena that looked as harmless as this one, not that Alshon was inclined to go easy. He believed that the execution of warrants set the stage for any investigation and were the primary vehicle for brow beating the accused into admissions of guilt.

He surveyed the quiet, affluent street. He wasn't fooled a minute. For all he knew, this Jeff Aiken had gone off his rocker and booby-trapped his house and office. It had happened before; it would again. He also didn't know if anyone was inside, ready to act out a final desperate scene of murder and suicide. No, it wasn't likely but then it did when it happened.

So Robert Alshon stood on the sidewalk with considerable satisfaction and watched the U.S. Marshal SWAT team execute the subpoena with the precision of a military operation. They wore imposing black combat fatigues, black helmets with bulletproof visors, bulletproof jackets, and brandished assault rifles.

"Not like the old days, is it?" Hubert Griffin said, walking up beside him. A neat, spare man, he'd disdained wearing the Windbreaker. Griffin was the U.S. Attorney who'd walked the subpoena through the court that morning while Alshon lined up the SWAT team. This was not the first time they'd worked together, and the tension was apparent.

"You're reading my mind."

"I see we're drawing a crowd."

Alshon spotted several neighbors standing just outside their front doors, arms crossed or holding a cell phone to an ear or using it to film them, all watching intently. That should be illegal, in his view. Law enforcement had every right to conduct its affairs without public scrutiny. That was one reason he preferred late-night/early-morning raids, but time worked against him in this case.

His attention was drawn by shouting from the inside of the town house where Aiken lived and worked. "Clear!" was repeated in different voices.

Alshon accepted that he'd learn little today. What he wanted was on the computers and for that he needed Susan Flores. She knew what to look for. Speed was essential at this point. Aiken would be tipped off at any time if experience meant anything. That was why he'd acted so quickly with the subpoena. It was a lesson he'd learned the hard way.

The muscled U.S. Marshal in charge of the SWAT team came out, carrying his helmet in one hand, his weapon in the other. "No one home, Mr. Alshon," he said. "We're checking for bombs right now. We'll be finished in a few minutes and you can send your people in."

Alshon looked back at the van parked behind the SUV he'd arrived in and gestured with two fingers. The side door immediately popped open and a team of five stepped out, ready to go. He'd not previously worked with them as they worked out of the D.C. office. He'd told them his expectations and the urgency he'd conveyed was apparent in their demeanor.

Ten minutes later, the U.S. Marshal in charge gave the all clear. His deputies exited the house, entered two SUVs and one van, and drove off, as the search team entered. "Shall we?" Griffin said.

Inside was surprisingly neat and orderly given that the target was a bachelor. The town house was carefully divided between living and work space. The team was already at work in the well-illuminated office, which had been the living room. Within minutes, the computers were being carried off to the vehicles along with exterior drives, discs, thumb drives, anything that could hold information or serve as a backup. There was no need for Alshon to give instructions, tell them to take everything. They knew that. The place would be stripped bare before they left.

It was true he didn't really need it all. Taking the suspect's personal effects, his clothing and intimate items was intended to set the tone of the investigation. And possessing them placed Alshon in a strong psychological position.

"I made a call this morning," Griffin said tentatively, moving delicately to the side to let a young woman wheeling a file cabinet pass. "This Aiken has an excellent reputation. Have you looked into his background yet?"

"No. There's been no time. The Exchange's IT report is pretty conclusive on its face," he said. "This is almost a formality. I'd just like to find something linking him to the brokerage account or find evidence of other, similar acts."

"You know he used to be with the Company."

"Of course." The antipathy between the FBI and CIA was well known in government, and while Alshon might now be with the SEC, he'd started with the Bureau.

"I'm told he's primarily responsible for uncovering Operation Pandora. You know about it?" Griffin asked. Alshon shook his head. "Those Saudi brothers in Paris who tried to bring down the Internet and planted destructive viruses in computers. They were all set to execute on the same date. There were a number of deaths."

"That's not really my area these days. I might have read something somewhere."

"It was hushed up so the full extent of the effort isn't common knowledge. They didn't want the public to know how close those two came to causing really serious harm." Griffin paused, then said, "You remember that alert on integrity issues with your computer content?"

"Which one?"

"About two years ago. It was the one that said there was a virus that could change the content of documents in your computer, told you to confirm facts of any doc you received by e-mail before acting on them."

"That one. Yes, I remember it. It's been a pain, I can tell you."

"Well, I understand this Aiken guy discovered it and alerted us."

Alshon hesitated, then said, "Even if all that's true, he wouldn't be the first patriot to decide to make a buck illegally."

"Yes. You have a point I suppose."

Alshon grunted. "He probably wrote the code, then claimed to find it so he could play the hero."

"I'm just saying that this guy's done his country a service. We should look carefully at our evidence."

Alshon eyed him steadily. "I intend to do just that and don't need to be lectured about my responsibilities. I've got a chartered flight to take all this stuff to my office. My staff will be up all night working on it. I'll have him before this is finished."

"Oh, I don't doubt that."

"Sir, there's a security system," the search team leader said to Alshon. He pointed to two discreet cameras.

Alshon stared at them as he processed the information and considered ordering the system disabled. "Leave it. We're executing a subpoena, not burglarizing his house." And the harm was done. The security company would likely alert Aiken, probably by some automated system. He'd know at once what was going on. Well, he had what he came for and there was nothing to be done about that now.

"Yes sir. We're moving upstairs."

"Fine. I'll wait here." Alshon checked his watch. Everything was by the book so far. If it stayed that way, he'd be back in his office in New York before ten. Then, he thought, then I'll nail the bastard.

28

From somewhere down a long corridor, Jeff could hear his name. It was muffled, distant, like when he'd been in school and a faraway friend was calling out to him.

"Jeff. Jeff. You awake, big guy?"

Reality struck like a solid wall, or a speeding car. One moment Jeff was interacting with the gossamer existence beyond himself, now his world was filled with bright colors and sharp sounds. He heard the insistent beeping of an electronic machine. He could smell odors, not like home, like a hospital. He opened his eyes.

A man was in front of him—two of them, actually—but they were just alike, moving together though speaking with a single voice. "It's me. Frank. Are you tracking yet? You came around a bit ago, mumbled something that made no sense, then drifted back into la-la land. The nurse said they want you awake now, so wake up."

Jeff blinked his eyes, then blinked again as he tried to clear his vision. The two images merged and there was one Frank, blurry but a single mass now. "Water." His voice sounded old, as old as he felt.

"Oh, right. I should have thought of that. I always come out of a coma parched. Here you go." He lifted the water to Jeff's lips.

Jeff drank, water never tasting so good. He finished the cup.

"Easy. I'll give you more in a bit. How much do you remember?"

Jeff thought. "I was running. I think. Maybe I was planning on running. I'm not sure."

"You were in Central Park, running. What happened then?"

"I don't know. I had a stroke? I fell? Got mugged?"

"Now you're getting there. You were attacked. How's that for New York luck?"

"Attacked?"

"Yeah. Witnesses told the cops a man jumped out of the brush and attacked you with a heavy stick or club. He just missed. You jumped the railing and bolted onto the street. The cops think you were going to a cop car parked there but a car hit you on the way."

"A car? I don't remember that. Or any man."

"The driver was late for something and was pushing forty. He just winged you but you were thrown in the air and banged your head really hard when you made a rough landing. They were worried for a bit and want to run some more tests on you now, but the scans and such say you're okay."

"My whole side hurts, and my arm."

"Frankly, you're lucky to be alive. It was a really close call. Your forearm's not broken but it's going to hurt like hell for a bit. Are you seeing double?"

"Not now. Before."

Frank beamed. "That's excellent." He poured more water and held it to Jeff's lips.

This time Jeff didn't finish the glass.

"You know," Frank said as he put the glass down, "this is no accident. I mean, I guess the car hitting you was sort of an accident but not the attack. Mugging a runner? You didn't have anything on you worth stealing. No. Someone was gunning for you. You mug people out on the streets near an alley. Whoever it was wanted you."

It took a moment for his thoughts to gel; then Jeff said, "You think it's connected to what we're doing now? That doesn't seem likely."

Frank shrugged. "We're both Company so obviously it could be related to that. It's never entirely out of my mind. But you've been gone quite a while, plus you worked in the dungeon and were not a case officer. But unless you've got enemies you've never mentioned, my best guess is that it's related to our current work. When we last talked, you told me you think the code is related to trades. Do you have any idea how much is involved?"

Jeff thought about it. "No. But it could be a lot."

"If it's in the Exchange's software, it will be a lot, but it doesn't have to be that much to make it worthwhile killing someone."

A trim nurse wearing too much makeup entered just then, and Frank moved away from the bed to give her room. She smiled at Jeff and made friendly talk as she checked the machines beside him. "No sign of bleeding on the MRI," she said with a smile. "And that's really good news. I'll bet you're going to have a headache for a few days, though. You took a hard knock."

"Anything I should worry about?" Jeff asked.

"Not a thing, honey. You just relax. The doctor will be around in a bit. He wants to run more tests. You can ask him questions." She moved his pillow a little, then adjusted the sheet.

"I don't want to wear you out," Frank said when it was just the two of them again.

"I've felt better."

"The report's finished from my end. I caught Stenton in the hallway earlier, and told him what happened. Maybe I should wrap this up tomorrow, unless you want to put it off until after you get out of here."

"How'd he take it?"

"Frankly, he acted like he didn't believe me."

"That we penetrated? Or that we found a rogue code?"

"Either one."

"That seems odd." Frank shrugged again. "Go ahead and give him your report, tell him I'll follow up with him after I'm out and feeling better, see if there is anything else they want us to do."

"I wouldn't count on that, Jeff. He's not the only one acting funny there. It's like all of a sudden I'm not welcome. Oh, your stuff's in the top drawer over here. You can check messages when you feel up to it. Your phone's been vibrating almost nonstop."

Jeff reached over, the motion taking great effort, pulled the drawer open, and took out the cell phone. His home security company had been calling every five minutes for over an hour. "Hang on," he said. He brought up the automated message, and it went to video. There were men and women in his town house in Georgetown. They were cleaning out the place. "Jeezus," he said. "Someone's broken into my house." He handed the phone to Frank.

After a minute, Frank said, "Yeah, look at the jackets. SEC. I think that's what they call executing a search warrant."

"A search warrant? Why would they do that?"

"I'm not certain, but I've got a hunch." Frank paused as his thoughts raced, then, "We need to act, then we can decide on options. If you don't think you'll die on me, I suggest you start getting dressed while I make a call or two. You don't want to be at a location they know about, if you know what I mean."

29

Richards Iyers went to the vending machine in the break room. He'd begun to feel better, the deep fatigue he'd earlier experienced slowly disappearing. His apprehension had also faded, evolving into a mild uneasiness. He chose a Coke, wanting the sugar and caffeine. He opened the can, took a swig, and scanned the room. Spotting Rose, the office gossip, he joined her.

"Did you hear about those two?" she asked immediately, almost as if she'd read his mind, leaning forward, her voice lowered to a conspiratorial level.

"Which two?" Iyers answered, suppressing a sense of excitement. To his great surprise he'd heard nothing all day, either about what happened at Central Park or the two mystery men who'd been working on their floor these last weeks.

"Jeff and Frank." She lowered her voice. "They've been stealing."

"Really? How do you know?"

"Everyone knows! They were hired to do a pentest but IT found out that after they got in, they'd been emptying accounts." Though officially confidential, major IT referrals to the SEC had a way of leaking into their department almost immediately. This was no surprise given the relationship between the SEC and NYSE IT security.

"They got in? You mean they penetrated to the core code?"

"That's what I heard."

"That's not good. Someone's going to get in trouble over that."

Rose blanched. "You think so?"

"I do. Especially if they used the access to steal. Is the SEC on it yet?"

She leaned even closer. "I heard they did a raid in Washington today."

"A raid? That's pretty fast."

"I guess there's a lot of money missing and the SEC was concerned they'd take more if they were left free."

"I saw their office was empty earlier."

"Right. I think they were arrested. We just haven't heard yet." Rose's eyes were wide.

"That's really something."

At his desk, Iyers accessed the jump server. To avoid the audit logs, he used the cover of the first stage of the new trading engine deployment. For the next hour, he scanned, searching for whatever alerted IT. When he found it, he smiled.

Campos. He'd done this. It was a bit bold, but he was glad to see the man stepping up. Planted in the system was malware very similar to the one used in Vacation Homes only this one rather blatantly manipulated trades at a steady rate that was bound to attract the notice of the security programs searching for just such behavior. After a few minutes, Iyers saw the code was moving shares into a brokerage account set up in the name of Jeffrey Aiken. Iyers cringed at that, thinking it too obvious. No one would believe Aiken would be so blatant.

But think whatever he liked, IT had bought it. On reflection Iyers realized it was so obvious they had to. It was not the way Iyers would have gone about it, but he had to admit it got the job done. He just hoped Campos had covered his tracks because once Jeff and Frank were in custody they'd deny their guilt. They knew what they'd done in the system and if allowed to, they could walk a skilled programmer through their process. After that, Campos's hack work would stick out like a sore thumb. If an impartial investigator seeking the truth put his mind to it, he'd conclude pretty quickly that the two men were set up. And that would lead in a direction Iyers didn't want to think about.

He grimaced, then closed his eyes. He should have made sure he killed Aiken when he had the chance.

30

Jonathan Russo left the staff meeting and made his way back to his office largely unhappy. Since the disaster on Monday, his team had yet to find an answer. For all the talk during the meeting, they had no idea what had gone wrong with their new algo. The old one was still operating without issues, but that was small consolation. And though his team believed the new algo was fine, that was what they'd thought up until the moment they'd launched it. The fact that they were unable to discover the problem was not reassuring and Russo had refused the tentative suggestion they relaunch it without a change.

"That's real money we lost," he'd pointed out, "not Monopoly play money. And we can't tolerate another hit such as we had Monday. We need to understand what went wrong. If it's our code, let's find the problem and fix it. If it was something outside, something beyond us, we need to know that as well, so we can take measures to see that it doesn't happen again. I'm not adverse to some level of risk, but we need answers." Alex Baker, his chief assistant, had agreed with him, urging caution as well.

When it was clear they were no closer to a fix now than they'd been the previous day, Russo gave instructions to put all their limited resources on the Toptical IPO coming the following Wednesday. Like most HFT companies, Mitri Growth had long planned to exploit the launch. An IPO of this size, with this level of excitement, was tailor-made for them.

For one, there would be an enormous trading volume and each block of trades presented an opportunity for profit. The sheer size also made it easier for their orders to lurk in the computers unobserved. They weren't doing anything wrong, certainly nothing illegal, but scrutiny was undesirable and you could never predict when the SEC might suddenly decide that a common HFT practice was now against the rules. It had happened before. A high-profile IPO such as Toptical's was just the event when they might make such a decision, especially if something went wrong and they were looking for a company to blame.

The other desirable aspect of such a high-profile IPO was that the stock was all but sure to rise initially. There was always a level of pent-up demand for high-profile companies going public and though the underwriters appeared, once again, to have made too much stock available, the price was likely to increase in the early trading. In Twitter's case, it had just kept rising. It was a situation ideal for one of Mitri Growth's special HFT algos.

But as the Facebook IPO had proved, the stock could be overpriced, which meant that within a short time it would begin to fall. This was a less desirable possibility for a high-frequency trading company, but there was still a lot of money to be made selling short, especially once the pattern was set.

And their IPO algo was designed to make money in either direction.

The problem with short selling was that if too many traders got involved it became a self-fulfilling prophecy. Algos from different HFTs competed against each other for advantage at lightning speed. No one yet fully understood the consequences. HFTs had first caused, then exacerbated the Flash Crash with aggressive selling and actions intended to complicate the system, actions that quickly spun out of the control and comprehension of their algos.

Before computers, a broker made a bit of money on every sale, as did the Exchange. High-frequency traders now injected themselves into such trades, taking a small percentage of each transaction. Every high-frequency trader was in the game, and their numbers were growing every month. No one took a lot, but everyone took something. So when someone bought stock, it was as if the offer had to punch its way through a succession of invisible digital walls, each one thrown up by a high-frequency trader. It slowed the trade, skimmed money from the deal so that by the time it was consummated the buyer paid more than he thought he would, or the seller received less. High-frequency traders had taken the cream.

At first, the delays and amounts were insignificant but high-frequency trading was so profitable it continued drawing countless players, many of them offshore, shielded from scrutiny. Even Russo, who had thrived in the industry for years, had no true idea who many of the players were or, for that matter, the full extent of the holdings they put in play. There were rumors, accepted opinions, but in the end, it was all speculation. What he knew was that the delays and effects on pricing were now very noticeable to anyone paying attention. The trading public wasn't on to the scheme yet but those who made their living on the stock market knew and were increasingly leery.

Russo sat down at his desk and placed his face into his hands with a sigh. When he took this job, he'd failed to comprehend the pressure he'd be under. He'd thought his team produced the finest algos in their industry and still believed they did. But when something went wrong, as it had Monday, high-frequency trading had the capacity to drain money from the company like there was no tomorrow. He'd had a disaster already but if next Wednesday went the same way, Mitri Growth and his career would be ruined.

The problem, Russo had come to understand, was that all the high-frequency traders were acting in the same way. There was no need to exchange messages or read internal memos. They were all doing the same thing, playing on the same field with the same end in sight. Each of them might do something a bit different and occasionally one came up with a novel approach but essentially they were like sprinters. They wore the same shoes, the same clothes, bolted from the same starting blocks, and ran flat out. It was no surprise that most of them finished almost together.

And Russo realized that was the danger. High-frequency traders represented a majority of all trades and if they acted in unison, which was the danger when an IPO went south or had a glitch, the stock would begin to collapse, and the volume and the frequency of their trades could pile drive it into oblivion.

And it was an event like Toptical's IPO that presented the perfect occasion for that to happen.

31

Jeff eased onto one of the single beds more exhausted than he'd realized. For the last three hours, he'd been in a daze, led by Frank, first out of the hospital, then in and out of a succession of taxis, culminating in a subway ride uptown. They'd exited, walked three blocks, and checked into this cash-only hotel built from appearances at the turn of the previous century. Not that many years before now, it would likely have housed a den of crack dealers but then the area had been cleaned up. Now it was just run-down and management still asked no questions if your money was green.

"Do you want to eat?" Frank asked from across the small room.

"I'm not hungry." Jeff's head throbbed, his side ached, and his arm was ablaze.

"I understand. I need to go out and get you something for the pain. I'll pick up food and bring it back. We'll see then if you have an appetite. What you need most of all is rest. So don't fight going to sleep. We're okay here."

"Frank," Jeff said, closing his eyes, wondering if he had the energy to undress, "what's going on?" They'd had no time to talk in detail since they'd seen the SEC raid on his office and home in Georgetown. Frank had managed a call or two to contacts while Jeff quickly dressed in the hospital and received a callback in one of the taxis, but he'd not said anything before now, not wanting to risk being overheard.

"NYSE Euronext IT made an SEC referral on us. They think we used our access to the system to steal from accounts."

"The Exchange is accusing us of theft when all we're doing is helping them secure the system? That's ridiculous!"

"Yes, it is. But the SEC has to act. They don't know how honest we are." He grinned.

"Why didn't they just talk to us? We could show them what we've been doing, answer any questions they had."

"Maybe at one time that's what they'd have done but things happen so fast now, they felt they had to move first and ask questions later. Do you know Robert Alshon?" Jeff shook his head, regretting it at once. "He's a senior SEC securities investigator. Ex-FBI. He's the pit bull on our case."

"Why don't we just contact him and explain things? Or do it through an attorney, if you think we should."

"We need to know what's going on, Jeff. Right now, we're in the dark. If we go to him the way things are, it's like lambs to the slaughter. He's undoubtedly got evidence we know nothing about. We need to find out what he has first, so we know what questions to answer."

"I guess."

"There's another side to this you need to keep in mind. It's a sad commentary on the state of affairs—but sometimes they don't care if you didn't do it."

Jeff suddenly felt numb. "What do you mean?"

"There's a mind-set in federal law enforcement that everyone is guilty of something, so everybody deserves what happens, even if they didn't exactly do what they're accused of. The laws are so far-reaching, so subject to interpretation, they can be made to fit most any scenario. And when it comes to Wall Street, that's a labyrinth of its own that allows them to justify almost anything they want. The juries don't understand. They take the government at face value. And your lawyer will tell you to cut a deal rather than risk trial. Just look at what they did to Aaron Swartz."

Aaron Swartz had been a cyberstar prior to his death at age twenty-six. An Internet pioneer, writer, political activist, and programmer he'd been involved in the development of the Web's feed format RSS, part of Creative Commons and also Reddit, a popular social news site. He was an outspoken critic of government and corporate control of the Internet. In 2010, he became a research fellow at Harvard University but that didn't spare him. In early 2011, he was arrested and charged with two counts of federal wire fraud and eleven counts of violating the Computer Fraud and Abuse Act for simply sniffing data off of MIT's network from a computer hidden in a closet on its campus. He hadn't shared or profited from the files he'd stumbled on. Facing up to fifty years in prison, forfeiture of assets along with a one-million-dollar fine, he was in line to serve a greater sentence than someone convicted of manslaughter, bank robbery, or rape. He hanged himself. Jeff had never considered that someday he'd be in much the same position.

"But we haven't done anything wrong!"

"So we say. That's what all the guilty types claim. They've heard it all and believe none of it."

"By running we look guilty."

"Jeff, Jeff. We look guilty already."

After a minute, Jeff said, "So now what?"

"First, I need to find out more. Our stuff's back at the hotel. I'm going out to see if I can get it. They've moved fast with this subpoena, but we've moved fast too and they won't have expected that. I doubt an arrest warrant's been issued for us. They're probably planning on picking us up at work in the morning. Assuming they knew you were in the hospital they'd have gone for you there." He reached into a pocket and extracted a thick packet. "Here." He laid it on the table.

"What's that?"

"That's six thousand dollars. I've got a bit over four with me. I may need some of it before the night is over."

"Cash? What are you doing with ten thousand dollars in cash?"

"Jeff, you amaze me at times, you really do. I never go on an assignment without cash. It's the first lesson I learned at the Farm and in ops. Never leave home without it. This may be a plastic age, slowly turning digital, but cash is still king, especially when you go to ground."

"Why would you need to hide out?"

"It's been well over a decade since I last needed to, but once you're in that mind-set, you never lose it. It's like learning to look both ways before crossing a street, a lesson you would do well to take more to heart. It's an instinct. And now"—Frank gestured by spreading both hands to take in the high ceiling, drab room—"you see why."

Jeff eyed the money. "What'll I do with it?"

"You'll figure that out if I don't come back. At least it gives you an option. Now, listen. I've taken the batteries out of our phones. Don't get foolish and put yours back in and make any calls, and for God's sake, don't use the room phone. There's nothing you're in any condition to learn right now. Just get well. I'll be back as soon as I can." He stood up and slipped on his jacket. "You need to trust me on this, Jeff. It's what I did for many years, and I'm still here to tell the tale. Now, get some rest."

After midnight, Frank quietly let himself back into the hotel room. He closed the door, secured the inside latches, then turned on the bathroom light so he could see what he was doing with the indirect light. He set two pieces of luggage on the floor, and a plastic bag on the desk, then went to the bed. Jeff was asleep. Frank touched his forehead. No fever.

As he laid the luggage on the stands and opened his suitcase Jeff woke. "So you're back. How'd it go?" His voice was drowsy, as if he'd awakened from a deep sleep.

"Not bad. I paid a bellhop to get our things. Probably money wasted. I never spotted anyone covering our rooms or in the lobby. I picked up some food if you're interested, hot subs. And I bought some disposable phones. This dump's got wireless, if you can believe it, so we're good to go."

"Do you know anything more?"

"I activated a new phone while waiting at the hotel and made some more calls to contacts from my former life. No one knows much, except this Alshon guy is known to move fast on occasion. We are apparently such an occasion. I called Stenton at his home."

"Wasn't that risky?"

"I ditched the phone."

"What did he say?"

"He didn't want to talk, said something about us violating his trust, and told us to turn ourselves in. At least it confirmed what we already thought." Frank sat down, pulled something out of a paper sack. He laid it on the dressing table and began unwrapping it as the inviting smell of food enveloped the room. "Sure you don't want something? Smells good."

"I'm not hungry."

"Fair enough. Don't mind me. Go back to sleep." Frank took a bite. When he could talk again, he said, "In a bit I'll check if our backdoor is still up and see what I can see. Maybe get an idea of what set the Exchange's IT off." He took another bite. "There's something else." He looked over at Jeff. "I called Daryl and asked for her help."

There was no answer. Jeff was sound asleep.